BET On Us

A story in the world of
With My Whole Heart

MariaLisa deMora

Edited by Hot Tree Editing

Proofreading by Whiskey Jack Editing

First Published 2019

ISBN 13: 978-1-946738-56-1

DEDICATION

For those readers who demand more.
Thank you for the encouragement.

Contents

ACKNOWLEDGMENTS

Almost as soon as I closed the manuscript on *With My Whole Heart*, I dreamed of writing Trent and Jacob's story. But it wasn't until months later, during an early morning breakfast with fans-to-friends Megan, Chris, and Sandy, when I found my "in" with these characters. And that *in* wasn't actually with them, but via a long-lost sister and an unknown nephew.

I hope you enjoy this story of unbreakable love and poignant loss. It turned into so much more than I expected, because we're graced with not one, but two couples exploring the boundaries of their love. At very different places in the arc of their lives, these men are universally fearless in the way they move through tough and demanding situations.

Thanks always to the folks at Hot Tree Editing, headed by the fearless Becky, as well as Mel with Whiskey Jack Editing. Your insightful comments helped clarify thought, tidy dialogue, and made the story better.

Woofully yours,
~ML

Bet On Us

Jericho Conway is the type of son most people would be proud of. He doesn't cause trouble, keeps his head down, does whatever's asked of him, contributes to the family, and doesn't talk back to his mom. They've been on their own for as long as he can remember, and he's always done his best to take care of her—lately that's in spite of his stepdad.

Jericho's a way-too-mature-for-his-age fifteen (and a half), and he's feeling stuck in the small community outside Knoxville where they live. Stuck, because no one here is quite like him. He's different from his classmates, has been all his life, but what sets him apart is one of those secrets that can't ever be brought to the light of day.

Then his stepfather stumbles onto his secret. And Jericho's right. There's hell to pay.

Eeerrrrkkk. <--That's the sound of a screeching halt.

Okay, okay. As the person writing the description, I know *Bet On Us* might not sound like a totally romantic story right off the bat, but it really is! On the one hand, there's Jericho himself. He's amazing, promise. And strong, so very strong. Then we've got his uncles, who would do anything for him. In Trent and Jacob, we get to see this dynamic, resilient, and loving couple with deep family ties, especially when you factor in Jacob's sister and her family. (That's Jaime, Connor, Nate, and Matt from *With My Whole*

Heart. Oh, and Jordan, Nate's best friend.) Jericho is finally exposed to the kind of fierce and loyal example for how incredibly sweet love should be, and thinks he might see an echo of the thing that's always set him apart. Here's hoping his Coming Out Day gives this precious boy exactly what he needs.

Continuing on …

It's been two years since Trent first watched his husband's eyes grow misty as they talked seriously about babies. Two years of Trent and Jacob searching for the right clinic, then the right surrogate, and then the ever-elusive "right time." However, all of their tentative plans come tumbling down when Trent receives a phone call from his hometown. A place he'd long ago left in his rearview mirror, stuffing all the memories associated with his personal Coming Out Day into a deep, dark hole never to be revisited.

Only now, Trent is forced to return, because the call is about the murder of his estranged sister and the health and welfare of a half-grown nephew he didn't know existed. Thrust into guardianship of Jericho, Trent and Jacob struggle to help the damaged teen deal with his grief and the hidden reasons behind his mother's death.

Chapter One
Jericho

Jericho watched as his mother turned tear-filled eyes towards the man who'd just pushed past the sea of gray hospital drapes surrounding them. In a motion he'd seen her perform a million times, she wrapped thin arms around herself, defensively crisscrossed as if she anticipated a destructive blow she wouldn't be able to ward off, not this time. As if when the strike finally landed, she'd burst into shards of wounded woman and had to proactively hold them together.

Frank Stemp turned his head side to side briskly, as if there might be hidden combatants in the corners of the tiny cubicle. With a hateful gaze drilling into Jericho, his stepfather gritted out a question aimed at his mother. "Why the hell did you have to bring that whining brat to the ER this time, Estelle?"

The anger in his stepfather's growled question reverberated through Jericho's bones. He knew that the man's anger disguised fear of being found out, and Jericho ducked his head, staring down at the ice bag a nurse had given him earlier. The numbing ice had helped with the pain somewhat, sure. But right now, holding the soft cloth in place was a valid reason to keep his arm covered up. If Jericho didn't have to look at the evidence of his stepfather's hatred, the terror swamping his senses would have time to ebb, flowing away like sand.

His peripheral vision picked up movement, and Jericho jerked his gaze up as his mother stepped between them, shielding Jericho behind her in an unexpected change from previous tactics. "Mom?" She flapped a hand at his trembling question. He knew in his gut that her challenging Frank was a mistake, but he was tired, and hurt, and chose to subside rather than insist she back down from whatever line she was drawing. *This isn't gonna end well.*

"You got something to say to me, Estelle?" Arrogance and rage warred for space in Frank's voice. "I can tell you that anything other than 'I'm hella sorry' comin' out of your pie hole right now, it ain't gonna sit well with me."

"You broke his arm." She hissed the accusation, and Jericho angled his head to see around her, focusing on the anger morphing into an unbridled rage on Frank's features.

"I did not." The bald lie rang with false conviction as Frank flashed a dare over Estelle's shoulder to Jericho. "Boy got a little bitty bruise. He's clumsy as hell. You know how he is, Stella." *Go ahead*, it seemed to say. *Go ahead and call me a liar. See what that earns you.* Jericho already knew exactly where that would lead him, and it wasn't a path he particularly wanted to walk again.

"Frank."

Jericho sank backwards on the table, gaze once again fixed on the shifting surface of the ice pack. If his mother was resorting to single statements of her husband's name, then the argument was already over. He imagined they'd be leaving the ER in a few moments, Frank's arm around Estelle's waist, Jericho trailing behind them.

Experimentally, he curled his fingers as far as he could, biting down on his tongue when the pain tried to expel as a grunt. Not broken in two, because he could turn his wrist a tiny bit and wiggle those fingers, but the injury to his arm was far more than just a bruise. Jericho lifted the ice pack and peered at the flesh underneath. Red and white in sections, the colors raised by the chill of the ice weren't able to hide the black-and-blue stained outline of four fingers and a thumb.

His mind flooded with the memory of how it had all happened.

"Boy?" Frank's voice shook the rafters of the barn, and Jericho fumbled with his pants, yanking them high on his thighs and then into place as his fingers worked the fastening at his waist. Desperately trying to shove the other evidence of his activities under the pile of loose hay off to the side, he fluffed the yellow straw unevenly across where he'd hidden the magazine. "Boy?"

The thudding stride of Frank's boot soles hitting packed dirt came closer, and Jericho knew he had to answer soon, or he'd get the belt for ignoring Frank. He scanned the area one final time and sighed in relief. "Yes, sir?" His call was quiet, but it was enough. Frank would be able to hear him and pinpoint his location. Pitchfork in hand, he was prepared when Frank appeared in the doorway of the stall and had just bent to scoop a pile of hay. He shook the pitchfork gently, letting the stems sift through the tines of the tool, as if he were looking for a final, errant horse apple. "Yes, sir, Mr. Frank?"

Elbow on the hinge post, Frank glared down at Jericho. "What are you doin', boy?"

Jericho let himself look puzzled, knowing the denser he played his thinking, the better Frank felt about himself. It was a strategy that had derailed a lot of lessons in the past, and one Jericho had worked hard to refine. "Mucking stalls?" The uplift on the end of the sentence might have been a bit much, because Frank's scowl deepened. "Sir. Was there something else I'm meant to be doing?"

"What's that?"

At the brusque question, Jericho couldn't stop his glance towards the incriminating piles of hay. Gaze darting back to Frank's face, he saw the man's attention wasn't on the innocent-looking stall floor but on the back waistband of Jericho's jeans. Straw stuck out in clumps, the prickly ends pointed every which way. Now that it had his attention, Jericho felt the stinging itch of raised welts caused by a combination of dust and scratches from the sharp shards of plant matter.

If he'd played dumb earlier, he aimed at dumber now. "What's what?" He gave another half-hearted poke at the hay along the edges of the stall, lifting, shaking, and sifting to find nothing. "I'm almost finished here, Mr. Frank."

"You take me for a fool, boy?"

Jericho wanted to shout yes, but he kept his response to a mute headshake as Frank took a pair of steps into the stall, swinging around behind Jericho and yanking at the waistband of his jeans. Startled, Jericho pulled away, and Frank overbalanced as he lost his grip. As if in slow motion, he watched while Frank's foot came down on the pile of hay, that innocent-looking mound of straw that crinkled underfoot in an unnatural way.

Neck bent at a deep angle, he saw the sweep of Frank's boot as it cleared the camouflage away, revealing the glossy colors of the cover, the young, painted face that stared up at them pouting prettily for a red-lipped kiss. With his heart pleading for a retreat with every quickening beat, Jericho watched as Frank meticulously cleared the straw away with the side of his boot, ensuring the entire magazine was on display.

"What the hell is this?" Frank sounded completely bemused as he bent at the waist, movements stiff and awkward, performing a hesitant dance as his arms swung free, fingers first grazing across the paper as if to convince himself it was real, then tentatively plucking at the corner

to peel it back. The next two pages were an ad for a dance club in Knoxville promising "More man meat on display than anywhere else in Tennessee." Neck still bent awkwardly, Frank slowly turned his head to look at Jericho, and the expression on his face wasn't horror, or even rage as expected, but a dark desire that silted Jericho's blood with fear, causing his heart to hammer faster in his chest. "That the way it is, boy?" Frank straightened as he spoke, until his back was ramrod stiff and he could use his full height to tower over Jericho. "That the way you like it? I didn't break you of that perversion yet?"

"Not for lack of trying." Faster than a thought, the response was on and across Jericho's lips, set free in the air between them before he could curb the words. He watched as they hit true and saw Frank's pupils darken at their shared memory.

About five years before, Jericho had been visiting the son of a new-to-the-county family that had moved in just up the road. The little boy, Edam, had been twelve, just around two years older than Jericho, and he'd gone along with the boy when he wanted to play touching games.

That time, their not-quite-innocent activity had been what his brand-new stepfather walked in on. Frank's severe version of punishment had been meted out over months and months, any time it came to the man's mind. Jericho had been unable to writhe away from the lash of Frank's doubled belt, the fold catching him around the groin and buttocks until at times his little penis had been purple from the bruising, butt cheeks and thighs burning red from the repeated blows.

Jericho's mother had somehow put a stop to it after the only time she'd witnessed Frank's cruelty. She'd paid dearly for intervening and told Jericho later not to cry over her bruises. "It's a momma's duty to protect her son."

If only she'd done a better job of it.

Frank reached into his pocket and pulled out a short, fat cigar. One of the stinky-sweet, home-rolled stogies he bought at the tobacco and vape shop in town, spending cash freely even as he gnawed on Jericho's mother's ass any time she needed money for the house.

Staring at Jericho, Frank clamped the cigar between his teeth while he dug for his lighter. A few flicks of the flame later and he pulled deep on the cigar before plucking it from his lips. He blew a thick column of sickly smoke towards Jericho. "Which hand, boy?"

"What?" Jericho clutched the handle of the pitchfork in front of his chest, unsure what Frank wanted from him.

"Which hand do you use to jerk off to that perverse shit?" Cigar back in his mouth, Frank puffed madly until the ember on the end glowed cherry red. "Which." Smoke wreathed his head, making him look like a demented demon wearing hell's version of a halo. "Hand." Frank lunged towards him, and Jericho's right hand betrayed him, instinctively slipping behind his back, away from the monster standing far too close. Frank's voice lowered to a hiss as he whispered, "Gotchu."

Pitchfork forgotten, Jericho lurched towards the open door of the stall, pulled back by an immovable force gripping his arm. There was a yank and a twist, and he became a ragdoll whirled in a circle. His back slammed against the wooden wall as pain ripped through him, centered on his forearm. A red curtain descended on his vision until he was nearly blind, barely able to see Frank's face pushed close, silent mouth moving around the cigar clenched between his teeth.

Frank had left him lying on the straw. He'd stared down at Jericho as the teen sobbed, arm cradled to his chest, then stalked to the magazine, where he'd viciously stubbed his cigar out in the middle of the cover model's forehead.

The pain in Jericho's arm had leashed him to the floor, making every movement agony, and it had taken long minutes until he could rise to his feet, the stench of smoldering paper filling the air. He'd carefully stomped on the magazine to ensure no sparks remained before gathering it and the pitchfork in one hand to make his way out of the barn.

By the time Estelle had gotten home from work, Jericho's arm was swollen to twice normal size. She hadn't spoken, just stared at him as he recounted his carefully crafted tale of clumsiness. He'd closed his eyes against the sight of her bright tears and sat quietly in the straight-backed kitchen chair as she moved around him to the linen drawer. Still wordless, she'd fashioned a long sling out of a flour sack dish towel, tying it carefully behind his neck.

At the ER, a compassionate nurse and no-nonsense doctor had listened to Jericho's recounting of his afternoon, shared a dark glance between them, and then left together. That had set off a quick bustle of activity, with ice and juice arriving, carried in with a promise of X-rays and pain relief. The next entry to the little faux room had been Frank, not quite half an hour later.

"Come on, Mom." Jericho sighed and reached for the sling his mother had made. "If it was really broke, they'd have been back by now." Shifting towards the edge of the gurney, he held the sling out to her. "Help me get this on."

"Good to see one of you has some sense." Jericho cut his gaze up to Frank's face, acid boiling up his throat at the self-satisfied look the man wore.

Before he could slip off the wheeled bed and to the floor, there was a commotion in the distance, rapidly coming closer. A mass of footsteps. Jericho heard heavy booted treads interspersed with the soft-soled shoes the nurses wore and one pair of heels, clickety-clacking their path up the hallway. The gray curtains boiled with movement before they slid to either side, much like the curtains of the one high school play Jericho had gone to last year. Positioned in the opening were the nurse, the doctor, and a new face—one petite woman carrying a briefcase. They were ominously backed up by two bulky policemen who stood farther back in the hall.

"What's this?" Frank's surprise came out angry, and that tinge of fear Jericho had heard earlier broadened until it took up almost all the space in his voice. "What's going on? What's the meaning of this?"

"Mr. Stemp, Mrs. Stemp, I'd like you to come with me." Firm and decisive, the authoritative voice didn't issue from either cop but from the woman who barely came up to their shoulders. "The doctor will take care of Jericho."

"What do you mean?"

Frank's outburst rode roughshod over Estelle's softer, "I'm not leaving my boy."

The woman swiveled to face Frank directly. "I have some questions for you, Mr. Stemp. I'd like to conduct my interview in a room the hospital has set aside for our conversation." She took a step backwards and gestured towards the hallway with a swing of the black briefcase. "If you'd come this way, please."

The nurse had edged around the cops and was beside Estelle, arm over his mom's shoulder as the nurse whispered urgently into her ear. Jericho's mother looked over at him, and he watched as a tear broke free from each eye, tracking down her cheeks. "I'll be right back," she promised quietly, and Jericho nodded. Her head was bent near the nurse's as they walked out of sight.

One cop had positioned himself behind Frank, and Jericho watched as his personal nightmare's head swiveled back and forth, trying to keep an eye on each of the policemen. The doctor appeared as if by magic beside Jericho, and the arm laid on his shoulders felt simultaneously too heavy to bear and so light it could float on air. His nose tingled and the room swam around him, swooping in big circles while his ears filled with the wild buzzing of a thousand bees. He blinked up at the ceiling tiles overhead, realizing the doc had somehow scooped his knees up and deposited him prone, back in the middle of the gurney.

"Breathe for me, Jericho. Shallow breaths in and hold, hold it, son. Okay, breathe it out slow. Do it again." Jericho followed orders, surprised when the buzzing and tingling receded rapidly, leaving him panting and sweating. He looked around to see the gray fabric walls had been pulled back into place. Everyone else had gone, disappeared, leaving only the doctor remaining with him.

"Where's my mom?" He tried to push up but used his injured arm by mistake. "Oww. God *bless* that hurts." Arm cradled to his chest, he stifled a whimper as he stared at the doctor. "Where's my mom?"

"She's talking to the social worker."

Okay. That's good. Jericho'd known what coming to the ER would most likely mean. Before leaving the house, his mom had gathered up clothing for both of them, stuffing it into a pair of plastic store bags and stashing them behind the seat of the car without a word to the oddness of her actions. She'd known the cascade of events coming their way, too, and had prepared for this outcome. "When do I get to go with her?"

In his mind, the answer was clear. Once Frank was out of the picture, they'd be okay. It'd be tight financially until Jericho could quit school to start working legally, but he'd already been hauling hay and working around the farms in the surrounding communities, so he knew he could pull his own weight. It was mid-June, and school had ended for the year, which meant he had more hours to work, too. The boarding business he'd started already brought in steady money, and he had faith they'd survive whatever kind of financial hit it'd be to lose Frank.

"Son." The consoling tone of the doctor's single word jacked with Jericho's breathing again, as the untimely shared load of pain and sorrow bore down on him in a wave.

"No. No, no. See, she didn't do anything. It was Frank. I'll tell the cops that and it'll be okay. It was Frank." Saying those words aloud felt more freeing than anything else he'd done. "Not my mom, never her. You saw where she was when you came in here. Between him and me. She protects me. It was all Frank. Every time."

"Jericho, how old are you?" This doctor, whom Jericho had initially liked because it seemed like he didn't take any guff off anyone, leaned back against the single hard wall, arms folded across his chest. Right now, in the middle of whatever this was going on, his no-nonsense manner no longer seemed like a good thing.

"Fifteen." He paused a second and swallowed. "And a half. I'm small, but not a kid."

"Fifteen and a half." The doc waited for Jericho's nod. "You're old enough to get the real deal straight. You with me?" Another long pause until Jericho let his chin dip again. "It's late on a Friday night, there's only one social worker on call, and she's already talking to your mom. If she determines your mom is the best place for you right now, then you and your mom will go to a shelter."

"But the barn, the horses—"

The doctor shook his head, dismissing Jericho's concerns as if they were dust motes on the air. "If she determines your mom isn't the best solution for tonight, you'll go to the group foster home here in town." The buzzing was back, and Jericho knew he was breathing fast. "Don't get upset. It's not as bad as it sounds. The judge will be presented with the case on Monday, and he'll sort everything out."

"No, my mom needs me. She's not well a lot of the time. She can't muck or feed. The dust makes her sick." Jericho shook his head, pleading with the doctor to understand, praying the man would somehow become an advocate with the power to make what Jericho wanted real. "She needs me. It's Frank that's the problem, not her."

"That's not for me or you to decide, Jericho. My job is to set your arm, make sure you're healthy, and ensure your safety. That's what I'm going to do. You're safe now, son."

As if, he thought, bracing for pain as the doctor reached towards his arm. A nurse breezed through the drapes, two small plastic cups in her hands. One held a pair of white tablets, and Jericho wordlessly put them in his mouth, chasing the pills with big gulps of water from the other. He climbed off the table and into the wheelchair when told, sat on the short stool in the X-ray room while the tech clucked over him like a momma hen. Then to the casting room, where the doctor met him again, and to Jericho's relief, so did his mother.

He didn't ask her anything, put off by the look in her eyes that promised *later*. The pills threatened to make an unwelcome reappearance when the doctor rotated his wrist, and Jericho had to breathe through the nausea. He swore he could feel the bones in his arm grinding together, the pain sharp and sudden as red descended upon his vision for the second time that day.

In the end, he got to walk out of the hospital alongside his mother. Jericho managed to hold himself together until they were in the car and he realized he couldn't pull the door closed, not with the cast on his arm. Not with his fingers like fat little sausages stuck on his hand. Not with the pain. Not feeling weak and small, chemically distanced from the events of the day. With tears in his eyes, he leaned out to try to grab the door handle with his other hand, but as he clipped the doorframe with his elbow, the cast made a hollow *crack.* The jarring blow caused him to cry out.

"I'm sorry," he told his mother when she came around to close his door. "I'm sorry."

"Oh, Jerry. I'm sorry, too." She cupped his chin in her hand, fingers brushing away his tears. "We're gonna be all right now. I've got a restraining order." Jericho blinked up at her. "Means he can't come on the farm at all. You and me, we're gonna be safe from here on out."

An eerie echo of the doctor's words, and they stirred the same silent retort in him. *As if.*

Chapter Two
Trent

"Jakey," Trent called, pitching his voice to carry throughout their house. "We've got to get a moooove on it, lover." Bending at the waist, Trent Conway smiled as he plucked his husband's socks and briefs from the floor, balled them up, and tossed them into the laundry hamper sitting three feet away. Jacob Grimes usually left a trail of clothing behind on his way to bed every night, and after so many years together, Trent had given up trying to convince him it was worth the effort to do differently. If the clothing remained on the floor, they'd be joined by a second layer, then most likely a third before Jacob felt compelled to straighten up after himself.

Footsteps in the hallway had Trent standing upright just in time to watch Jacob walk through the door. *Five feet ten inches of hunka hunka and all mine*. "There you are, honeybuns. Did you get snacks packed?"

"Babe" was the entirety of Jacob's rejoinder, and Trent rolled his eyes in mock frustration.

"Oh my God. You didn't. Jakey." He stepped close and had to wait no time at all before Jacob's strong arms bracketed his sides, hands cupping an ass Trent knew was round and firm, just the way his Jakey liked it. "Not gonna work, big guy."

"Oh, yeah, it is." Jacob's smile tilted crookedly to one side, and amusement gathered in the lines at the corners of his eyes. "It always works." He angled his head as he came in for a kiss, pushing up to meet Trent's descending mouth. The scrape of Jacob's scruff was still a delicious thrill, soft lips providing counterpoint sensations. Then Jacob parted Trent's lips, tongue delving deep into his mouth, and he melted into the kiss, giving way to the quiet moan rising from his chest. He deliberately set aside any annoyance, focusing instead on the sensations swirling within him from the close embrace. *I've always been a sucker for making out with him.*

The abrupt ring of a phone sounded in the background, but Trent ignored it, wrapping his arms around Jacob's shoulders and pulling him closer. It sounded again, then quieted, and he renewed the kiss.

Until the phone rang again, the loud and grating ring-ah-ring shaking him free from the lust-filled haze blanketing his mind. Staring into Jacob's eyes, Trent wanted nothing more than to take his husband to bed and disregard the call of responsibility. "I should get that." Jacob's lips twitched, and he shook his head, pulling Trent's head back down until their lips touched. "Jakey."

"Trentie." Jacob's tongue traced the edges of Trent's mouth. "Kiss me, fool."

He couldn't ignore the dare in Jacob's voice. Jacob had done it knowing how hard it was for Trent to not jump when the phone rang, one of the non-awesome side benefits of being his own boss. He never knew when the call might be from a big, new client, and making himself available was one way he tried to stand out from the hordes of developers who seemed to make the West Coast their home.

Jacob kissed him gently. And again, this time adding a vibrating moan as their lips touched.

"No really. I should get that."

"Uh-huh." Jacob's fingers curled around the arch of Trent's ass, gripping and pulling until their hips were pressed together. "In a minute."

"In a minute?" His voice was pitched two octaves higher than normal, and Trent whined piteously when Jacob ground against him. "I'll get it. Yeah, then." He tipped his head to the side when Jacob's grip in his hair demanded the shift in position, sighing when Jacob's mouth hit the side of his neck, teeth and lips working at his skin. "Oh, Jakey."

"Love you." Jacob's words were nearly lost in the rustle of clothing being adjusted. "So much, babe."

"Want you." Trent groaned when Jacob's fingers curled around him, aligning their cocks in his hand. "Feels so good." The phone trilled, signaling a voicemail message.

"Gonna get you off, babe."

Trent was wordless but not silent, mouth open as he made the sounds he knew Jacob loved to hear. No matter how long they were together, Trent would never get used to the masterful way Jacob handled him. As the bigger and slightly older man in the relationship, most outsiders believed he must be the papa bear to Jacob's cub. Nothing could be more wrong.

Wrung out by his orgasm, expertly caught in Jacob's hand and spread along both their dicks for more lubrication as Jacob brought himself to peak, Trent held tight to Jacob's shoulders while he fell apart, ejaculate dotting both their stomachs. When Jacob's chin tilted up and he demanded "Kiss me" without even opening his eyes, Trent was happy to comply.

"Love you, Jakey."

Jacob's lips moved against Trent's, and he knew his husband was smiling. "Love you more, babe." With a final sweet kiss, Jacob pulled back. "We made a mess."

"It's a good mess." Trent swiped a splotch of semen with one finger, bringing it to his mouth and sucking it off with relish. The salty flavor burst across his taste buds, leaving him wanting more. "So good."

Jacob's eyes had darkened and his voice held a touch of a growl when he warned, "If we're going to the clinic's picnic at all, you need to not get me riled again."

"The picnic." Trent had lost himself in the moment, completely misplacing the event they'd been getting ready for. He glanced at the clock on one nightstand and groaned, dropping his forehead to Jacob's shoulder. "We're officially late. Not gonna be late, but *am* late as of now."

"Don't care," Jacob declared firmly, dragging a roughened fingertip up the underside of Trent's cock.

"Well, you didn't want to go in the first place." Trent walked over and rummaged through the cabinet in the attached bathroom and found the softest washcloth they owned. "There's enough time yet. We can still go." He had his chin tucked as he ran the water, watching the splashing liquid race across his temperature-testing fingers, so he didn't see Jacob moving in behind him. The voice in his ear was barely preceded by a wave of body heat against his back.

"Let's not and say we did." Jacob shoved Trent's shirt up, and he lifted his arms helpfully. Then Jacob's hands stretched across his belly, fingers following his treasure trail down. Jacob's mouth was on his back, teeth scraping across one shoulder blade. "Let's stay home, babe."

Trent watched him in the mirror as Jacob methodically broke down all his defenses and arguments. He knew when to throw in the towel, so he turned to face Jacob, warm wet cloth in hand, and set about cleansing them both. The picnic was for a local surrogacy agency and clinic, intended to be a kind of icebreaker for couples looking at the process as a possible fit. The center's support group would be there, signing couples up for ongoing meetings to discuss successes and failures, providing a venting ground and a celebratory ally in one. After looking for the right agency for two years, Trent felt certain this one was the perfect fit, and he'd dropped paperwork off earlier in the week. That was when he'd found out about the picnic and sold Jacob on the idea. Of course that was a couple of days ago, when they'd been mid-vegging out on the couch and a picnic sounded good—not post-orgasmic and ready to collapse.

"Okay. But—" He gripped Jacob's cock and lifted, gently swiping at the base, smiling as Jacob groaned. "I pick the binge series today."

"Babe, you can do whatever you want as long as you keep touching me like that." Jacob's chin lifted. "You shatter me in all the best ways."

Trent leaned close and mouthed Jacob's neck, savoring the sounds he pulled from him. "Shattered, huh?"

"So shattered." Jacob's whisper was scarcely audible. "Gonna need a horizontal surface soon."

Finished with their cleanup, Trent gave him a final, soft kiss. "Bed or couch, you pick." He pulled Jacob against his chest, tucking the smaller man's face against his neck.

Pressing his lips to the crown of Jacob's head, he said, "I'll find you."

The look of love on Jacob's face was worth any number of missed outings. *Worth anything in the world.* Trent watched him saunter from the room, gaze on Jacob's swaying ass. *He is my world.*

Hanging the wet cloth over the towel hanger in the bathroom, Trent studied his own face. It was no shock to find the same soft look on his features.

In the distance, he heard audio from the TV in their living room and smiled, knowing the comfortable couch had won Jacob's decision on where they'd spend their evening. On his way there, Trent snagged his phone. Navigating the hallway on autopilot, he thumbed over to the voicemail application to see who'd called earlier. His footsteps slowed as he saw an unfamiliar number with a familiar area code.

Knoxville, Tennessee.

Cold sweat prickled across his shoulders. Trent only knew one person in Knoxville, a place he'd left behind nearly two decades ago with no more than a rusted-out car and the clothes on his back. In the intervening years, he'd returned only once, and found the same cold-shoulder lack of welcome.

Standing at the end of the hall, he looked across the room to where Jacob was curled on the couch. Blowing out a deep breath, Trent tapped the message and put the phone to his ear. Silence, then a light static, then a deep male voice announced, "Trent Conway, this is Alan Reedman from the Knoxville DCS offices. Please call me back on a matter of utmost urgency." Reedman recited a phone number, then said, "Again, this is Alan Reedman from the Knoxville Department of Children's Services, and I'll be waiting for your call."

"Babe, anyone home?"

From the tone of Jacob's question, it couldn't have been the first time he'd tried to get Trent's attention. He looked up, staring through Jacob as he intently listened to the message for the third time.

"You get a new client? You're so focused I wasn't sure you were still with me." Jacob sat and pointed the remote at the TV. The sound muted, and in the following silence, Trent was acutely aware of his heartbeat, pounding out a beat that nearly drowned out the voice still speaking into his ear. Jacob, now alarmed, barked a brusque, "What's up?"

"I—" Trent licked his lips. "I gotta make a phone call." He turned abruptly and walked quickly to the kitchen, leaning an arm on the island as he dialed. Footsteps behind him were all the warning he needed before he felt Jacob's heat press against his back, strong arms going around his waist. Silent support, no matter the need, and that right there was why Jacob was so much the better man than he was. Trent knew he'd be spouting off a dozen thoughtless questions, demanding to know who Jacob was calling and why. His insecurities were something he tried to hide, but they came out at all the worst times. Jacob was steady and patient, kind and adoring, and always, always certain of Trent's love.

"DCS, Reedman speaking."

"Mr. Reedman?" Trent tried to strengthen his voice, aware it was shaking badly. "This is Trent. Trent Conway." He paused, but the other man didn't fill in the silence, leaving Trent to blunder on, his nervousness growing with every breath. "You called. Me, that is. You called me. I'm not certain why, it's the weekend. Not that I mind. Your call. But it's late. Not here, of course, we're three hours behind. So it's late there." Jacob's arms tightened around his waist, and Trent pulled in a steadying breath. "Why did you call me, Mr. Reedman?"

"Mr. Conway, am I the first call you've received today?"

That was a strange question, and Trent pulled the phone from his ear, put the call on speaker and checked his voicemail. Only the one message from today. He looked at recent calls and saw there were two other Knoxville numbers that had called, but left no voicemail.

Laying the phone on the counter, Trent covered Jacob's hands with his, closing his eyes when Jacob threaded their fingers together. "I've got two missed calls from Knoxville, but no other messages. What's this about, Mr. Reedman?"

"Well, this puts me at an unexpected disadvantage. If you'll give me a minute, I'll conference in a colleague who can speak to the matter at a different level. I'll be right back, but before I do that, can you tell me if you know an Estelle Stemp, Mr. Conway?"

Hearing her name knocked the breath out of Trent. He opened his mouth, but nothing came out. A second attempt met no better success. Estelle. *Stella.*

"Mr. Conway?"

Jacob slipped his head around Trent's side and looked up into his face. Whatever he saw there made him understand the difficulty Trent was encountering. "Mr. Reedman, this is Jacob Grimes. I'm Trent's husband. He's got you on speaker right now. Can you tell us what this is about?"

"Mr. Grimes, if you'll hold on a minute, I'll get someone who can answer part of that question."

Silence from the darkened phone, and as they waited for Reedman to come back, Jacob tightened his hold on Trent's hand. "I'm here, babe. Whatever this is, I'm here."

Trent nodded, and they waited.

After an eternity, the speaker on the phone popped and hummed, then Reedman's voice came through. "Mr. Conway, Mr. Grimes, I'm back, and I've brought Trinity Chapman with me. She works for DCS but is a liaison to the Knox County District Attorney's Office, helping out when there are criminal matters."

"Mr. Trent Conway?" The woman's smooth voice paused, clearly unwilling to go forwards without confirmation.

Trent cleared his throat. "Yes. This is Trent Conway. I've got Jacob Grimes here, too." His voice was unfamiliar to his own ears, rough and gravel-filled. "What is this about?"

"Mr. Conway, Mrs. Estelle Stemp is your sister, is that correct?"

Jacob's head jerked, and he stared up at Trent. Trent had never hidden the difficulty with his family, nor the reason he'd left Knoxville in his dust, but he'd only spoken in very general terms about exactly what that family entailed. Trent knew if he'd talked in detail about Stella, or even acknowledged he had a sibling, Jacob would have pushed to contact her. His sweet husband was only capable of seeing the kind of supportive and loving relationship he had with his own sister, Jaime.

"Yes. Estelle, Stella's my sister. Is she okay?"

"Mr. Conway, I'm the liaison to the chief criminal investigator for the DA's office here in Knox County, and I regret to inform you that your sister was killed last night."

His arm gave way and he went to an elbow on the countertop, breathing loud in his ears. *Stella dead?* His eyes squeezed shut, and images of Stella danced across the darkness underneath his lids. Standing at the range in the family's kitchen, laughing over her shoulder at something Trent had said, looking carefree and vital. Clutching the dashboard of the sedan their grandparents had given her, face white as she taught Trent how to drive. Stella as she'd been the last time Trent had seen her, face twisted with anger and disgust, shouting at him to go away.

Forehead pressed against the back of his hand, he was aware of Jacob's voice as he took on the burden of talking to the voices on the phone, them answering, concern in every word while Trent warred for control within himself. A few minutes later, it was quiet once again in the kitchen, and Jacob molded himself against Trent's back, covering him protectively.

"Babe." Pain, deep and raw, bled through Jacob's voice, and at the sound, Trent's throat released the first sob.

Dark and painful, it ripped from him, followed by dozens more as Jacob gathered him up, turning him and steering Trent to the floor where Jacob wrapped him up, cradling Trent's head to his shoulder. Comforting and comforted, they sat like that for a long time as twilight crept through the windows, casting shadows in the corners.

Jacob stirred finally, adjusting his position with a groan. "Trent."

"Yeah." Trent sat up, swiping at the dried salt on his cheeks. Jacob looked nearly as wrecked as he felt, reflected agony in his gaze as he hurt for Trent's pain. "Should I call them back?"

"No." Jacob's answer was firm, and Trent appreciated him taking control of even just that. He felt scattered, bereft, and small. "I'll call in the morning when we know our plans."

"Our plans?" Trent swallowed, that action turning into another battle against tears as his chest hitched painfully. "Stella." He hated his voice like this, high-pitched and whining. Weak. "She's really gone?"

"How much did you hear?" Jacob's careful tone gave away the importance of the question. He climbed to his feet and reached down a hand that Trent took gratefully, letting Jacob guide him upright. "Beyond that first bit, how much did you catch?"

"Not much." Trent shook his head. "Nothing really."

A strong hand wrapped around his, and Jacob threaded their fingers together, pulling him towards the living room. "Come sit down." He winced and rubbed at his behind with his other hand. "Somewhere our asses won't go to sleep."

"Sorry," Trent said absently as he followed, eyes on Jacob's hand gripping his tightly.

"Come here," Jacob said, drawing Trent down beside him on the couch. "Your sister, Estelle."

"Stella," Trent corrected, then winced. "Yeah. Stella."

"Stella." Jacob lifted one shoulder. "Older sister?" Trent bit his lip and gave a single nod. "Trent, she was murdered."

"Murdered?" He'd heard "killed" and assumed accident. Stella murdered was beyond anything he could imagine or wrap his head around. "Who would do that? Who would kill her?"

"Her husband. They already know who. He shot her, then killed himself. Murder-suicide, the lady said."

"But why?" Trent's throat closed up again, choking off the last word. Stella murdered by someone who'd probably loved her was unimaginable. Through his tears he begged, "Why would he do that?"

"They didn't say. I don't know. But, Trent." Jacob took a deep breath in, one Trent tried to echo as if together they could bolster Trent's flagging control. "Trent, her son is why they called."

Trent stared at him. "That doesn't make any sense. Stella doesn't...didn't have a son." Trent had last seen her at their parents' funeral about six years ago. "I saw *him* once, the husband. But she didn't have a son."

"Yeah, she does, babe. No matter what she told you, Mr. Reedman was real clear. She had a son." Jacob's gentle words rocked Trent backwards. "Jericho. He's almost sixteen, his name's Jericho, and he needs you." Jacob's gaze was unwavering. "He needs us."

"Jericho." Trent tried the name out carefully. "Jericho Stemp."

"No, babe. Conway. Same as yours." Jacob's hand curled around the back of Trent's neck, his grip gentle but firm. "Same as yours."

"Jericho Conway. Who's his dad?" Trent stumbled over the question, intensely aware these should be questions he knew the answer to. "How old is he? Fifteen?

That can't be right. I saw Stella. Talked to her. She never said anything about a baby, a boy."

"His dad was killed in an accident when he was a couple years old. No relatives. Same on your side." Trent knew that. His parents had died, killed in a car accident. His own grandparents on both sides had passed away before that. "You're all he's got."

"What do we do?" He hated feeling so lost and uncertain, but he had faith Jacob would carry him through as far as was needed. "What did they say?"

"In a few minutes, I'll get the computer and book us seats on a flight out as soon as we can. I've got a couple names of folks we'll need to connect with, but we can do that easier in Knoxville. I'll call Jaime tonight, let her and her crew know what's going on. Trent, honey." Jacob leaned in, pressing his forehead against Trent's. "I'm so sorry. I know you couldn't have been close, but it's never easy losing someone, a sister, your family. Losing her at all, much less like this."

"Why wouldn't she have told me about the boy?"

"I don't know, babe. I just know what the guy said on the phone. Jericho's in the hospital and doesn't know about his mom yet. They're waiting on you to get there to soften the blow. So they need us there, and then we've got to be everything for this boy. Reedman said he was already working on paperwork so we can bring him home, but there'll be stuff for us to do once we're in town. Tomorrow's Sunday, so not a lot will happen until

Monday." Trent closed his eyes as Jacob's lips brushed his. "Every step of the way. I'm with you. We'll get through this."

"Will he want to come here?" Trent scoffed at his own question as Jacob's head rocked back and forth. "He doesn't have a choice, does he? God, that poor boy. I can't imagine how he's going to be feeling. If she didn't tell him about me, then even us walking in the door will be a shock." He fought through another round of weeping, throat so tight it choked him, stealing his breath. "I can't believe Stella's dead."

"Focus on what we can do, okay?" That made sense, so Trent nodded, then dropped his head to Jacob's shoulder, the angle awkward, but he needed the closeness, that comforting knowledge that Jacob would support him through this. "I'm going to look at flights. Gotta get the comp, so I'll be right back, yeah?"

"Okay." He straightened and stared at Jacob as reality sank in. His chest felt tight, as if his lungs couldn't expel all the air needed to pull in a deep breath. He fought with it for a moment, then bit back a sob. "We're all he's got?"

Fingers stroked across the back of his hand, and Jacob nodded somberly as he said, "Yeah, babe. We are."

That tightness in his chest twisted, turning painful as his heart clenched. *Stella's gone.* He had a nephew who was right now all alone in a hospital, probably afraid. Trent lifted his chin and stared into Jacob's eyes, finding everything there he needed to speak confidently. *He's my strength*. "Then we'll make sure he's got everything."

Jacob's smile was blinding, and Trent's eyes watered at the pride he saw in the face of his lover, his best friend, his husband.

"I love you so much, Jakey."

"Then it's a good thing I love you, too." They came together in a kiss that didn't demand, a caress that was soft and slow, and a reassuring exploration of all the things they already knew about each other.

His voice was husky as he agreed, "Yeah, it's a good thing."

Chapter Three

Jericho

The muted light in the room helped keep the headache at bay, but Jericho knew if he moved too much or too quickly, or even tried to sit up, his head would be pounding again. He'd already tried all of those things since waking in the hospital. On his back, with only a thin pad under his head, he stared up at the ceiling tiles, counting them for the hundredth time before switching the pattern and counting from the outside in instead of in rows. He couldn't read, not without risking a worsening of the headache, and even muted sounds from the TV had been enough to turn his stomach.

The nurse had let slip that he had a concussion, so he assumed the pain and nausea would lessen as it healed. A bruise on the brain wouldn't go away overnight, but if he mapped the ones on his ribs, he reckoned he'd be able to anticipate progress.

The cast on his arm felt heavier than it should, requiring more effort to lift and readjust positioning than was worth the limited amount of relief granted. His other hand had a needle stuck in the back of it, tubes connecting to a plastic pouch on a metal pole. Fluids, the nurse had said, and a way to give him pain meds without having to poke him every time.

Footsteps in the hallway got louder as they neared, and Jericho let his head fall slightly to the side, rolling his neck so he could look at the door. It opened slowly, and he saw Ms. Chapman standing there. She was the woman from the ER two nights ago. He'd talked to her once since, when she'd come to his room earlier, but only a few minutes into the conversation Jericho had started retching and she'd left him to the ministrations of the nurse. Behind her now were three men, and he quickly surmised none of them were police officers. They just didn't have the look. One was tall and thin, older, his skin darkened from years of sun.

The other two looked different somehow. Their clothes were nicer, brighter, hair styled just so. Jericho stared harder because the angle of their arms made it look like they were holding hands, and as they walked into the room behind Ms. Chapman, he realized they were. Two men in his hospital room, holding hands like a couple.

Did this mean the doctor knew about him? Had he called them here to talk to him, mentor him somehow in how to be gay? How could anyone know that unless Frank told them? Had Frank done this? Panic set his heart beating fast, and his headache followed quickly, pounding out a beat just over his eyes. Jericho could hardly hear over the racket in his head.

"Jericho, how are you feeling?" Ms. Chapman's voice was quiet, soothing in a way that made his nerves jump worse. "I've got something to tell you, and some folks for you to meet."

"Where's my mom?" He'd meant it to come out demanding, not puling like a kitten, but he knew a first grader could have done a better job. "I want my mom." The bigger man made a sound, and Jericho focused on him. Something about his eyes was familiar, but not, and Jericho stared. "I want my mom," he told the man before biting the inside of his lip, trying to stop the tears. "Where is she?"

"Jericho, how much do you remember from that night?" The tall man spoke up, then stepped closer and rested one loosely clasped hand on the foot of the bed. "Do you remember anything before you woke up in the ER?"

He'd already told the cops everything. More than once. Talking and talking until the nurses made them leave, because he'd been bawling like a baby, telling them about Frank and how he'd come to the farm. How he wasn't supposed to, because there was a restraining order, but he'd come anyway. He'd come and let fly with everything he had, not holding anything back, aiming to hurt and maim with every blow. That's what had earned Jericho the concussion, a vicious backhand to the jaw that had him flying backwards, his head connecting with the edge of a cabinet.

"The last thing I remember is Frank. Mom was in the barn because of my arm. She'd told me to stay in the house and she'd take care of the boarders. Frank was there and he wasn't happy." Jericho bit down hard until he tasted bitter copper, until the pain in his mouth was bright and overwhelming, until he'd pushed away the memories of Frank's shouts and fists. "The doctor in the ER said I hurt my head when I fell. That's all I remember." He swallowed hard, belly rolling ominously. "Where's my mom?"

Ms. Chapman stepped up next to the man and reached out, but she pulled back before her hand touched Jericho's leg. "Jericho, did you know your mother's family very well?"

The change in topics was confusing, and Jericho shook his head before he remembered not to, closing his eyes against the spike of pain between his temples. It took him a minute, but he finally wheezed out a quiet, "No, ma'am." He let that hang there for a minute, then gave her a little more. "I don't remember much about my grands. They passed a while ago. It's just me and Mom."

Shuffling footsteps came closer, probably the hand-holding couple looking to get the best view of the pitiful kid in the bed. He hated them for being there, for seeing him at his weakest, for inserting themselves into this thing, whatever it was, where they didn't have a place at all. Eyes squeezed shut, he waited.

A man cleared his throat, the sound gentle and soft. "Jericho, your mom, Stella? She's...she's my sister." Jericho turned his face towards the sound, like a cave rat seeking heat or food, or safety. "I'm... My name is Trent, Trent Conway. I'm your uncle."

"No." Jericho denied the man's words, not caring if that meant he called him a liar. "She woulda told me. She never had a brother." Something pressed into his hand, a fleeting touch of cold fingers quickly removed, leaving stiff paper in their wake. "What's this?" He didn't want to look, didn't want to see whatever proof this lying man thought to produce. "What'd you give me?"

"It's a picture of me and Stella on the day I got my license. She taught me how to drive." The voice was closer, even as other footsteps withdrew. With faint humor, the man continued, "She wasn't the easiest of taskmasters."

Jericho blinked as he lifted the photo, eyes slowly focusing in on his mom's teenaged face, arms propped on the shoulders of the smaller boy in front of her, chin on top of his head, both of them smiling broadly. The boy looked enough like her they could have been twins, and in his face, Jericho saw a clear resemblance in the features he saw in the mirror every day. Angling his head up, he studied the bearded face in front of him. Older, covered in beard, but the eyes were the same. Conway eyes, his mother called them. The shape and color, even the way they tipped at the corners were the same.

"Hey." The man's mouth moved in a way that said he was gnawing on the inside of his lip on one corner, something Jericho's mother did. A habit he had, too. "I'm Trent." He gestured towards the photo in Jericho's hand. "I've got more pictures with me, all from school and band. Ag club and stuff. High school, mostly."

"Why hasn't she said anything?" Jericho simultaneously wanted to shove the picture back and tuck it away for safekeeping. "She never said nothing about a brother."

"We had a falling out, years ago." Pain and an aching resignation crossed the man's features. Trent's features. "Something I've wished I could take back a thousand times. But us Conways, we're a stubborn lot."

Jericho stifled a snort-laugh at that, because it was the dead-set truth. He sobered and asked again, "Where's Mom?"

"Frank—" Trent's voice stumbled to a stop after Jericho's stepdad's name, and he held one hand out to the side. Jericho watched as the other man stepped up and took hold, their fingers falling between each other as if this was something they did all the time. Shock flooded through him, along with anger he didn't expect, and fear, because whatever had this man needing support had to be bad. "After he knocked you out, he went to the barn."

"No." Jericho snapped his lips shut after that single denial. *No, he left. He had to have.* That's what he'd been telling himself.

In an unsteady voice that ranged up and down the scale, Trent said, "When he got to the barn, he...he hurt Stella, Jericho. He hurt her bad."

Jericho shook his head back and forth, his intention of a single movement put to the side when his body continued its physical denial. *No*, he thought. *No, no, no. Don't do it. I'll hate you forever.* The pain in his head swelled, growing like a flash flood roaring down a dry creek bed.

"Frank wasn't, they don't think he meant to do what he did. Don't think he meant to take it that far." Trent stretched his other hand out, trembling fingers hanging in midair until Jericho surprised himself, reaching out and gripping hard, accepting the offer of comfort. Feeling small, with his hand swallowed by the much larger one of the man claiming to be blood, to be an uncle he'd never known, Jericho steeled himself for what was coming. Trent whispered what had to be truth—the fears Jericho had held inside himself after his mother didn't come to his room, didn't check on him, didn't come to find him. "He hurt her bad, then he did the same to himself."

"She's...are you sayin' she's..." Jericho couldn't bring himself to utter the words any more than Trent could, and they stared at each other for a long moment.

"He killed her, Jericho." Ms. Chapman broke the silence, her clipped voice drawing a line under everything Trent had been trying to say, everything Jericho wanted to deny. "We believe he thought you were already dead, knocked out like you were. Then he killed himself."

The last thing Jericho saw before tears filled his eyes was the sweep of devastation that crossed Trent's face, and as much as he'd hated him only moments before, Jericho felt sorry for him in that shared moment of loss.

Trent

"Then the guardian ad litem will petition on behalf of the child." Trinity Chapman was all business when discussing the legal ins-and-outs of Jericho's future, unlike when she'd shown a depth of empathy earlier in how she'd spoken to the boy. *The boy. Jericho. Stella's son. My nephew.* Trent was having problems following her and understanding what it all meant. "All told, we're talking four, maybe five."

"Days?" Trent winced. "We won't even have Stella, Stella's...the body. Back. For a funeral, I mean."

Chapman shook her head, face settling into those compassionate lines, her expression telling him he wouldn't like what she had to say. "Months, Mr. Conway. Four or five months."

"Before we can take him home to California?" Trent stood there, mouth open, not wanting to believe her. "Months?"

"Before he can live with you." She lifted her briefcase and popped a snap on the side pocket, pulling out a piece of paper. "He'll go into foster care when he's released from the hospital."

"Foster care?" Trent turned to stare at Reedman, whose mouth had hitched to one side like he'd tasted something bad, bitter. "Can that be right? I'm his uncle, and I'm here. I'm right here. That can't be right."

"Now, hold on, Trinity." Reedman stepped to the side and around Trent, squaring up against the tiny social worker. "Man's got a point. He's blood, and he's here. Dropped everything to come. I think we can sort things a bit differently."

"Alan." Chapman used a warning tone as she lifted the paperwork in her hand to shade her eyes against the stark sunlight. "Not a good case to bend the rules."

"What better case? Boy's lost his mother. We can't bring her back. He's got a blood relative standing here ready to be responsible for the boy. He's going to Conway in the end, either way. Why put the boy through the system if he doesn't need to be? Hospital's going to keep Jericho for another twenty-four hours, minimum; that'll count for a seventy-two-hour hold, and you know it would. If we don't put him in the system, then there's nobody to buck."

Chapman stared at him briefly, then bent her head as she stuffed the paperwork back into her briefcase, and Trent felt a moment of hope, because surely that meant she'd had a change of heart.

Reedman turned back to Trent and gave him a narrowed stare. "No chance your sister put you down as the boy's guardian in case of death?"

"Unlikely." Trent shook his head. "She'd have said something, I think."

"Mayhap you're right, mayhap you're wrong. I know the guy who is headed to the house tomorrow to turn it out—we'll get him to look in the Bible, in a fire safe if there is one, or in her bedside drawer. If we find anything naming you, then it's a done deal and transfer of guardianship is a court matter, not for DCS." Reedman nodded firmly. "Even if not, if Trinity here agrees that you're under the guidance of the courts, then we get you a lawyer and a judge. You'd have to stay until the probable cause hearing, but we can get that on the docket sooner since it's a different court." He took a step towards Trent and thrust out his hand. "Now, I've a dinner to get to. Pleased to meet you, Mr. Conway. My condolences on your loss."

Trinity Chapman offered much the same, and Trent watched the two walk away, Chapman not even reaching the tall man's shoulder.

A hand curled around Trent's, and he let himself sag sideways against Jacob.

"It's been a day, what?" Jacob's fingers squeezed and released, then wrapped around his waist. "Let's head to the hotel for a couple of hours. Then we can come back and see Jericho before visiting hours end."

"Did you see him?" Jacob made a noise in response, but Trent wanted confirmation. "No, Jakey. Did you see his face?"

"Looks just like his uncle. Those Conway genes run true, it seems." The hand at his waist tugged, and Trent started walking alongside Jacob. "You did really well, babe."

"Oh, God. His expression when he realized. I didn't think I'd survive." In front of the rental car, Trent turned to face Jacob. "She's really gone."

Jacob lifted his chin, and Trent pressed a gentle, closed-mouth kiss to his lips.

"She really is. But he's not. Jericho is so strong."

They separated and climbed into the car, Trent angling his seat back as he buckled the safety belt. He watched Jacob adjust the mirrors and smiled, because that changing angle was the third time so far. His husband was meticulous in some things. Trent let his mind drift as Jacob drove them to the hotel, only taking notice when Jacob was at his open door, hand out to help him from the car. Once in the hotel room, Trent stood for a moment, staring around at the bland interior.

"Jakey, is this really happening?"

Jacob's hand at his back urged him towards the bed. Beloved fingers tenderly undressed him, then coaxed him between the sheets. "You'll feel better if you can nap, even thirty minutes." Cheek pressed to his, Jacob whispered, "I'd give anything to make it have not happened, lover. Give anything to make this better for you." A kiss to his jaw, then his temple, then his lips. Trent curled onto his side and shoved a hand under his pillow. From just over his head,

Jacob told him, "Nap if you can. If you can't, then just relax. I'll unpack a few things and join you."

Eyes closed, he lay there and listened as Jacob moved around the room. There as a click and the sound of a fan that told him the toiletries were being unpacked, and he knew he'd find his shampoo waiting in the shower. This was one of the thousand ways Jacob took care of him, studiously taming his normally messy side and leaving behind a calming order for Trent. He blinked and watched as Jacob slipped shirts on hangers before tucking them into the closet. Not being quiet, nor noisy, just using an economy of movement Trent had always admired. He knew normally he was a little over the top, even a little campy sometimes, but Jacob took everything in stride.

"He looked at us holding hands." Unsure where the idea had come from, much less why his mouth decided to blurt it out, Trent went with the flow of thoughts. "More than once. Even before he knew about Stella, he noticed, and was...not shocked, exactly."

"Yeah, more like he couldn't believe we were being open about it." Jacob came and sat on the edge of the bed, reached out, and folded his hands around Trent's. There was silence for a few moments, then Jacob asked, "What was your actual coming out like? You've talked in broad terms that it wasn't good, and I never wanted to push. I got that it was a painful subject, and with my own issues with family outside of Jaime, maybe I didn't want to make you relive something that has the power to hurt so much."

"James is wonderful." Trent defended his sister-in-law stoutly, a little ache in the center of his chest as he thought about Stella. "She loves you, no matter what."

"Yeah, she does." Jacob's mouth twitched. "Loves you, too. When I brought you home the first time, she pulled out all the stops, didn't she?"

That had been in Memphis, where Trent had met Jacob. They'd both worked at a national ad agency and had been picked to be part of a project for a new client. The firm might not have gotten the business, but Trent got Jacob out of the deal, which he counted as a lifetime win.

"She did. Made her famous taquito casserole." He turned his hand in Jacob's grip and gave his fingers a squeeze. "I didn't know you'd walked in there expecting a fight. Had no idea that you hadn't told her you were gay. She was awesome about it all."

"Well, it hadn't gone well with the folks. Dad had spouted the 'no son of his' line and hung up on me, and Mom just cried." Jacob bent close and pressed his cheek to Trent's. "After that, things had just gone sideways until I met you. When I realized you and I batted for the same team, and then you agreed to go out with me? I thought James would be okay with it, but I chickened out at the last minute and didn't call her."

"Mine was different from yours." *Understatement.* Trent pressed a kiss to Jacob's jaw. "My dad threatened to kill me, and my mother offered to help him. Stella—she just stood there and let it happen. She was my big sister, my hero, and she just stood there while they said the vilest things. I turned and walked out and never looked back."

"How old were you?" Jacob's voice was soft, tender. "Babe, why did you never tell me?"

"Seventeen. And I didn't want you to… So many kids have it worse. I figured out what I had to do and managed. Sleeping on couches for the last three months of school so I could graduate, I worked my way through my friends until I'd worn out my welcome with all of them. At least my folks kept their mouths shut about why they'd kicked me out." He tried to stifle a shudder. "It was the things they said that caused nightmares. My dad going for the closet where he kept the scattergun. That and how my mom looked at me, like I was disgusting, a bug, something to be repulsed by."

"So, with Jericho, you think he's heard the same things?"

"It's very likely he was raised in an environment that didn't foster an appreciation for equality." Trent tried for a laugh, but it fell flat. "We'll have to take it slow with him, maybe cut back on PDA until we get an idea what his beliefs are."

Jacob sat upright, his expression puzzled. "I'm not going to stop kissing you and hugging you. It's not like I jerk you off in public, Trent. We tone it back as needed for whatever audience we have, but he's going to have to get used to it sooner rather than later." He pushed off the bed abruptly, stalking towards the minifridge. "You want a bottle of water?"

"No, Jakey." Trent felt chastened, and while he understood Jacob's reaction, it didn't make it hurt any less.

Jacob made his way to the other side of the bed and sat, taking a long drink from the chilled bottle of water before he placed it on the nightstand. Phone in hand, he fiddled with the screen, setting the alarm. Trent waited, knowing from long experience that Jacob wasn't done with their conversation. He would be gathering his thoughts, marshaling his arguments, and composing a defense that Trent wouldn't be able to withstand. But Jacob's voice was quiet and uncertain when he asked, "You think he hates it that much?"

Well, that wasn't what Trent had expected. He closed the distance between them, curling himself around Jacob where he perched on the edge of the mattress. Head on Jacob's thigh, he looked up to find an expression of confusion and hurt on Jacob's features. "I think I don't know much about him at all. I think we saw him at his worst today, physically and spiritually wounded to the bone. I think he's sad and confused, because it sounds like he and Stella were on their own, and he's old enough to know even estranged family is better than no family, so why she wouldn't tell him about me is anyone's guess. I think..." He paused when Jacob's fingers carded through his hair, neck arching so he could press into the touch. "I think he's a little lost boy right now, and we're the island in the distance he's not yet sure is real. We'll see how it goes when we head back." Jacob's fingers moved over his scalp, the gentle pressure grounding and sure. "Regardless, he's ours now."

Jacob's smile was as tentative as Trent expected. "Yeah, he is."

"Set the alarm and come give me a cuddle." Trent pursed his lips and smacked loudly. "Pappa wants his cubbie."

Jacob shoved his head away with a laugh. "Oh, fuck you with that cubbie bit."

"That'd work, too." Trent smiled at Jacob's laughter as they came together in the middle of the bed. "That'd work, Jakey."

Jericho

Uncle.

He massaged the skin of his forehead with the fingertips of his single good hand, trying to scrub away the questions that had been flooding through his mind every waking moment since the revelation. Not that his mom was dead, because Jericho knew he'd already come to that realization long before the legal and familial contingent had strolled through that door. There'd have been no other reason for her to stay away when he was hurt or sick. *She might not have had a good radar when it came to men, but she was a good mother.*

He blinked hard and swallowed around the knot forming in his throat.

Mom's dead.

He'd found he didn't want details, not right now. *Maybe not ever.* If he didn't know, then it couldn't eat at him, how terrified she must have been. Slowly, patiently, piece by piece, Jericho built up a scenario in his mind. One where she never saw it coming, where it was fast, so fast she didn't know anything. There and gone in an instant. No suffering. No fear. No crying out or last words. Just gone in a way she'd never be coming back.

Briefly he wondered about Frank, and then decided he didn't care. Part of him hoped Frank's death was cold and slow, painful and full of fear. The other part of him was just relieved he'd never have to deal with the man ever again. A memory of Frank's face as it had been in the barn that last day flickered and faded, the horrifying aspect of imminent torture at his hands gone forever.

Footsteps in the hallway outside signaled visitors of some sort. His room seemed to be isolated at the end of a wing, and the nurses' shoes were silent enough he seldom heard them coming. Jericho was briefly tempted to play possum, feign sleep so whoever it was would go away, but since the strides didn't hold the telltale tapping of heels, he suspected he knew who it was. He was suddenly struck by fear that he'd never have another chance to make a better second impression.

Uncle.

The specter of being taken from his mother had always been in the back of their minds. He knew it was one of the reasons she'd settled for Frank, because until the incident in the barn where officials got wind of the man's cruel hands, having two adults meant a buffer separating her and Jericho from the rest of the world. *Why didn't you tell me, Mom?* Family could have made all the difference in the world.

Focused on the doorway, it took Jericho a moment to realize the footsteps had paused, stopped short of his room, and he wondered if he'd been wrong. Then the two shadows on the floor of the hallway came together and merged into one, finally breaking apart after a long time. *They're kissing*, he thought. *But they don't want me to see*. The shadows were still for another moment; then the footsteps resumed, and a moment later, there was a sharp rap on the door as his uncle rounded the frame and walked into the room. The other man from before followed him, and Trent's arm trailed behind him as if he'd only just dropped his hold on the man's hand.

"Jericho." They stared at each other for a long beat, and Jericho felt the weight of his uncle's intense scrutiny. "How's the head?"

"You're really my uncle?" Jericho heard the tremble in his voice and hated it, hated showing weakness of any kind. "I didn't dream that up?" Trent smiled, and it looked so much like Jericho's mother that his eyes stung. "Really?"

"Really. You're my nephew. *God*." Trent gave a chuckle that broke at the end. "You look so much like Stella. I look at you and it's like seeing her all over again. You're a Conway for sure." That speared a shaft of pain through Jericho's stomach, and it must have shown on his face, because Trent hurried to continue. "That's a good thing, Jericho. Promise."

"So what happens now?" As much as he'd wanted to beg answers to his questions earlier, a nurse had come in and given him more medications that had made him sleepy, so he'd drifted off to the adults talking and woken alone. "If Mom's really..." He swallowed hard. "If she's gone, what happens to me?"

"You don't have to worry about that." Trent drifted a couple steps closer to the bed. "Just focus on getting well."

The idea of not knowing was terrifying, but that lump in his throat had grown to choking size, and Jericho pressed his lips together, trying to quell the trembling he could feel.

The other man stepped around Trent, and Jericho noted how he brushed up against this unknown uncle, shoulders touching in a way that seemed to bolster Trent. "Babe."

For a horrifying moment, Jericho thought that was directed at him, the endearment something a more-than-friends friend would say. But as he continued, Jericho realized he was talking to Trent.

"He deserves to know. It can't be easy, stuck in here without any information for so long and then to have the rug jerked out from under him by the news." The man turned his attention on Jericho and offered him a subdued smile. "Hey, we didn't officially meet earlier, but I'm Jacob. I'm with Trent." He shrugged. "Kinda obviously, I guess." He paused, and when Jericho didn't say anything in response, continued. "We're here to help figure things out, but the one thing that doesn't need any figuring is that we'll take care of you. You're going to live with us because family takes care of family, and we...we just want you to know how sorry we are that this is how you found out about Trent." He gestured to the side. "And we want you to know we didn't know about you, either. If we had, we'd have been here for anything you and your mom needed. What Trent was trying to say is you truly don't have to worry about anything now, because we've got you. We're here, and we've got you."

Jericho dropped his chin and scrubbed at his forehead again, trying to drive away the fear and anger. *I can't be mad at Mom.* She was dead and couldn't defend herself or her decisions, and it wasn't fair to her. *But it wasn't fair to me*, he wanted to shout. *None of this is fair.* He lifted his head, and batting the tears from his eyes with the edges of his fist, asked the first question that came to mind. "So you're Jacob Conway?"

Both men laughed, Trent a little hysterically and Jacob with a long-suffering tone. "No, I'm a Grimes. Jacob Grimes."

"But you're—" Jericho ignored the twinge of pain from his arm as he used the cast to gesture between the two men. "Together, together. Right? Or not? Did I get that wrong?"

"We're definitely together-together." Jacob smiled at Trent, the expression on his face so loving and sweet something broke inside Jericho. A wall, one of the many his mother had accused him of building over the years, toppled and fell. "I married the guy, but we couldn't come to an agreement on how to hyphenate the last names. Did I go with Grimes-Conway, or did we do Conway-Grimes? So for now, we've kept things as they are."

"When you say I'll live with you, what does that mean?" He thought about his bedroom at the farm, his clothes and the few books he'd been able to squirrel away, keeping them out of Frank's sight because the man didn't see any value in something he considered nonproductive. "The farm, the animals, someone's got to take care of them."

"A lot has happened since we left here earlier." Trent was focused on him as he took the final steps to bring him beside Jericho. "That lady, Ms. Chapman, she called a little bit ago with some news." Jacob pulled a chair close to the bed and physically directed Trent to it, pressing on his shoulders to encourage him to sit. Trent reached and took Jericho's hand in his, holding tight as Jacob left the room. "She said the investigators found some paperwork at the farm."

Jacob came back in with another chair in hand, and he settled it on the other side of the bed, bracketing Jericho. Jacob sat and propped his elbows on knees, leaning forwards.

"What?" Jericho chewed on the inside of his bottom lip, waiting.

"Your mom, Stella. She had a will. Frank didn't, but since he didn't really own anything, that's kind of a moot point. How much did you know about their...relationship? The land and such?"

"We rented the farm. Frank never could hold on to money long enough to put a down payment on anything. The animals, the horses in the barn, they're all rent-paying boarders." Jericho laughed, the harsh barking sound echoing around the room. "Never had much."

"Your mom's will named me executor." Trent lifted his chin and stared into Jericho's face. "And guardian. Of you. So, it's what your mom wanted, too."

"Where's your place at? Have I ever seen it? Maybe Mom drove past one day?" Jericho wracked his brain. "Is it close?"

The two men shared a heavy glance, full of unspoken words, so Jericho was prepared when Jacob spoke. "No. No, it's not. We live in San Diego."

"California?" Snippets of movie scenes were the sum of his knowledge about California, and outside of geography telling him San Diego was south of LA, he didn't know anything about the town.

Another long and silent communication by the two men drew out the silence after his blurted question.

Jericho shook his head. "I...I don't think..." He made a fist inside Trent's grip. "I've never been anywhere but here."

"My sister lives in Memphis. That's where I grew up." Jacob's words didn't make sense, because what did his childhood home matter? "We've been talking about relocating back there. My parents scattered after their divorce, and I miss my sister a lot. Our jobs—" He smiled, a slow lifting of the corners of his mouth. "Trent and I work remotely, so we can literally live anywhere. I've got two nephews there that are growing up too fast, and I hate I'm missing out on that. We flew out here so we could get to you as fast as possible, but we've talked about driving back to California. That'd give us a chance to stop in Memphis and visit. Introduce you to your new cousins."

"My cousins?" The concept was foreign enough to be intriguing. After being without family for so long, they seemed to be coming out of the woodwork now.

"Well, yeah. Trent's your uncle, so that makes me your uncle, too. Means my sister has to be your aunt, and she's thrilled at the idea. So her two boys are your cousins." Trent gave Jacob a look, a fond eye roll followed by clearing his throat. "What? What did I do now, babe?"

Trent broke in, his rough voice riding over Jacob's. "What my husband is trying to say is, what would you think about living in Memphis?"

"When—" Jericho closed his eyes. It was easier to speak into the darkness. "When's my mom's... Do you know yet?"

"Three days." Trent's fingers worked his fist open and curled around Jericho's hand. Softly he said, "The doctor left a note that you'll be released tomorrow. If you want, you can come with us to help pick out things for the services. Flowers, the music, the…other things. Is there anything in particular you want for her? Clothes or jewelry?"

"There's a blue dress she likes a lot. Says it makes her feel pretty. It has yellow flowers on it." He tried to pull in a deep breath, but his chest jerked and hitched. "She likes daisies. Calls them a common flower with an uncommon beauty."

"That's a lovely thing to say." Jacob's voice was followed by a firm grip on his fingers sticking out from the cast. "I wish I could have met your mom."

Jericho shook his head side to side, eyes still closed, the safety of the darkness emboldening him. "She'd've hated you. Same way Frank hated me. Folks around here don't have any time for perverts." Trent's fingers spasmed and tightened around his hand. "His word, not mine. Sorry."

"Nothing to apologize for, Jericho. And it's nothing I haven't heard before." Jacob's voice was low and gruff, thick with emotion. "The only reason I'm willing to go back to Memphis is because my folks aren't there now." He gave a laugh filled with pain instead of humor. "I'm pissed that you've had to deal with that kind of hate, but I've heard worse, trust me."

"'Family takes care of family.'" Jericho repeated his words back to him. "Not always, huh?"

When he opened his eyes, blinking through tear-clumped lashes, he saw water tracks on Trent's face, but it was Jacob's expression that left the strongest impression. Through whatever painful memories he was fighting, Jacob had turned to look at Trent, and the love on his face was clear and true.

"Okay." His firmly stated word had them both looking at him, brows raised in near-identical expressions of confusion. "Memphis sounds okay."

Chapter Four

Trent

"Oh my God." Trent closed the hotel door and settled his shoulders against the firm surface. "Oh. My God." He leaned his head back, eyes closed. "The expression on his face, Jakey. Oh, my heart."

Jacob's hand closed on his wrist and, with a steady pull, drew him towards the bed. "I know, babe."

Trent opened his eyes as he stumbled to a stop. "It's bringing up bad memories for you." He knew all about Jacob's disastrous coming out to his parents. "I'm sorry, Jakey."

"No." The single word was firm, Jacob's denial unshakable. "Don't be sorry for me for anything. You know I'm a fan of karma, and I'd like to think the good life we've built reflects on me, on us. The sad lives of my parents, that's on them. But Jericho, there's no way he's deserving of any of this. Karma got it totally wrong for this kid, and it's up to us to help balance the scales."

"Can we do this?" Trent sighed, exhausted and feeling defeated by the enormity of the situation.

Jacob had seated himself on the edge of the bed, and Trent loomed over him. Jacob nodded fiercely, and Trent reached out to smooth dislodged hair back from his face.

Staring down at the man he loved with his whole heart, Trent sighed. "He's going to need so much."

Jaw set, Jacob said, "I don't think there is anyone on this earth more suited to helping Jericho through this and the upcoming years than you and me. Swear." He reached up and undid Trent's belt buckle, then the fastening of his jeans. "We're gonna take care of him, and that's just how it's going to be. Always, always bet on us."

Trent smiled at the expression on Jacob's face, tongue tucked into the corner of his mouth as he worked the teeth of the zipper down over Trent's hardening cock. He swayed as Jacob tugged at the waistband of the jeans, pulling them halfway down his thighs, followed by his briefs. Hand fisting in the hair at the back of Jacob's head, he tilted Jacob's face up even as a hand wrapped around his erection. Jacob's grin turned into his tongue sticking out, which turned into a saucy curl and swipe across his upper teeth. Tip to root, Jacob stroked him with a firm grip.

"This for you or for me?" Trent's voice trembled as he took in the vision before him. Jacob, love of his life, straining against the hold Trent had in his hair, mouth already open and ready.

Jacob twisted his head to the side and pressed a kiss to the inside of Trent's wrist, then looked back up at him. "This is for us, babe. Because I love you, and I never ever wanna forget how lucky I am to have found you."

"Pretty sure I found you," Trent teased as he relaxed his grip, keeping his hand gentle on the curve of Jacob's skull. Heat bloomed around the head of his cock as Jacob laved the crown before taking him inside. Fluttering touches of wet tongue tapped along his shaft as he watched himself disappear inside Jacob's mouth. Full, pink lips closed tight were the only warning he had before Jacob sucked, hard and demanding, fingers jacking Trent's cock. He was lightheaded as blood rushed to his groin, making him more rigid than before, the beating of his heart overshadowed by the greedy noises Jacob made. "Lover," he whispered, and was treated to Jacob's eyes rolling up, hair falling in his face while he blew Trent.

Jacob tugged on his sac, making his balls draw up hard and fast, tight to his body. Firm strokes along the raphe on his perineum led to his hole, and he gritted his teeth as Jacob teased him, fingertip circling the opening with intent. Trent shifted, widening his stance as much as he could, hobbled by the fabric of his pants. The pressure disappeared as Jacob pulled off his dick for a moment to slick a finger, then renewed, and Jacob's cheeks sculpted in as he sucked harder, tongue working the underside of Trent's cock. Trent pushed out, and his body accepted the intrusion easily; then he shouted a garbled warning as Jacob unerringly found his prostate.

His hips jerked forwards and back as, eyes closed, Jacob swallowed around him. The blissed-out expression on his husband's face was all it took. "Jesus, Jakey. Look at you." His cock swelled and pulsed, then shot deep in Jacob's mouth, Jacob's throat working as he swallowed. Trent's fingers again fisted in his hair, holding him in place. "Just look at how gorgeous you are. Jakey. Oh, Jakey. I love you. So much, honey. So much."

He eased his dick from Jacob's mouth, shivering when the movement pulled Jacob's finger from his ass, too. Fingers wrapped around the root of Trent's cock, Jacob licked and kissed his way to the tip, where he hummed as he placed a final kiss before opening his eyes and lifting his face to look up at Trent. Lips reddened, his mouth and chin wet, he smiled. "I love you, too, babe."

"I gotta sit before I fall down." Trent made good on his words with a laugh, twisting in place so he could fall to his back on the mattress. "Made me weak in the knees."

Jacob curled up against his side, and Trent hooked a finger under his chin, bringing their mouths together for a deep and wet, tender kiss.

"Want me to blow you?" He lay his head back with a sigh. "Handy?"

Jacob laughed, the sound so deep and smooth and well-known it made goose bumps raise the hair on Trent's arms. "No, I'm good. You think I can blow you like that and not get off? I'm the no-hands wonder, don't you know?"

Trent smiled up towards the ceiling as his eyes drifted closed. "I'm that good, am I?"

"So good."

They lay like that for several minutes, listening to the far-off sounds of traffic muted through the windows.

"We should get undressed." Jacob's mumbled words made Trent chuckle, because he sounded like he'd rather lie there together. "Get a good night's sleep."

"Yeah." Trent didn't move. "We should."

"You first." Jacob stretched and nestled his cheek against Trent's shoulder. "I'll go next."

Trent slipped his hand down Jacob's back and into the waistband of his jeans, stretching and pushing until he cupped Jacob's ass.

Then he pinched firmly.

Jacob shouted as Trent's planned rolling escape was thwarted by Jacob lying on his arm, and his husband's thrashing hadn't moved him away.

He pinched again, gasping when Jacob's fingers found his nipple.

"Don't," he pleaded, eyes already blinking away the expected burn. Then Jacob's mouth was on his in a slow, sweet kiss that ended with their foreheads pressed together. "Jacob," he'd just begun, intending to restate his love, when the burn hit, Jacob's fingers twisting brutally. "Ohmygod." He gasped and slammed himself backwards.

"Titty twister." Jacob chortled a laugh as he jackknifed from the bed. "I call dibs on the shower. My underwear is sticking to me."

"I hate you," Trent called after him, trying futilely to rub away the pain.

"Nah, pretty sure you love me." The door closed on Jacob's jaunty whistle, and Trent smiled.

"Pretty sure you're right," he whispered, lifting his head to see his nipple was as reddened and puffy as Jacob's lips had been earlier. "Ow."

Jericho

The car door beside him opened, and Jericho took a deep breath before swinging his feet out, planting them firmly on the gravel driveway. Looking up to where a tent rode the top of this slight incline, he saw a larger group than he'd expected milling around. Jacob stood just to his side, and Trent was in front of him, hand outstretched. Jericho pretended he didn't see it and stood on his own, immediately swaying as his head swam. It didn't matter, because as he was coming to know and believe, neither Trent nor Jacob would let him fall. Sure enough, one hand landed under his elbow, and another gripped his arm just above the cast. Either alone would have steadied him, but both buoyed him up.

"Thanks," he muttered, gaze downcast, studying the tips of his new dress shoes.

It was the second day after he'd been released from the hospital, and a lot had changed since then.

The hotel had been a revelation, Jacob somehow wrangling a suite where the two men had been staying in a single before, and Jericho's bed felt larger than his entire bedroom had been at the farm. The tiny soaps and bottles of shampoo had all smelled good, even if he couldn't shower because of the cast. Nearly a week had passed since he'd broken—since Frank had broken—his arm, which meant he had another five long weeks before the annoying and heavy plaster could be removed.

They'd driven from the hotel to the closest mall, and Jericho had dawdled until he was walking behind the couple, unsure of his place in this world they inhabited. They'd been careful about even touching in front of him, something he could see in the aborted movements of hands, the way Jacob always crowded close to Trent, and the looks they gave each other that he knew they thought they hid. Through the past two days he'd been wondering if it was just him they were afraid of, but watching them at the mall had shown him more of the same. There, even Jacob had kept his distance from Trent, arms crossed imposingly across his chest. The two men had shown up at the hospital earlier that day with new everyday clothing for Jericho that they'd bought at the local discount store. And the shoes and the suit Jericho now wore had been the fruits of that mall trip, with alterations to the one sleeve to account for his cast.

Being discharged had taken forever, and he didn't understand half of what the doctor had said to Trent and Jacob, but the earnest concentration in both men's faces had convinced him it was okay not to know. Just like that, he'd understood and believed that they'd take care of him. Then, once in the rented car, with Jacob driving and Trent turned halfway around to talk to Jericho, he'd directed the way to the farm. He'd swallowed hard as they turned into the drive, disoriented to see the yellow police tape flapping in the breeze, broken and disconnected in places so it became a buttery-colored snake trailing along the ground, twisting in place and threatening ankles with a good trip if he got too close.

It hadn't taken long to gather up the things worth keeping. The photo album his mother had kept, her family Bible. That wasn't where Jericho expected, and Trent had to explain that's where the investigator had found the will, that single piece of paper that handed responsibility of Jericho over to her brother, a man she'd kept a secret all these years.

He'd rounded the corner from his room into the hallway to see Jacob's back as he stood in the doorway of the room his mom had shared with Frank. "I don't know," Trent had hissed, and Jericho had slowed his steps, listening closely. "Do we need to get shoes for her?"

"The white sandals." Jericho's voice had cracked, and he'd cleared his throat, finding that lump had made yet another reappearance. "That's what she wore with the dress." Jacob had moved backwards to allow Jericho to shuffle in front of him where Trent was standing, dress in hand. "You found it." He'd looked at the nightstand on her side of the bed. "Her jewelry is there. She don't have much, but there's a necklace from her gramma that's real pretty."

His throat had closed tight, breaths coming short and shallow as he turned and walked away, shaking. By the time they'd left the house, he'd been covered in sweat, exhausted and sad, overwhelmed by how much life had changed. The boarders had all picked their horses up by then, and the silence emanating from the barn seemed charged somehow, as if the acts that had occurred inside had deadened the very air around the building.

Jacob had ordered room service once they'd gotten settled into the suite, and Jericho had wondered how he could have gotten everything so right without even asking. Trent had made contented sounds as he ate his roast chicken, while Jericho had battled his burger until Jacob had taken it from him, cutting it in half without a word. He'd dropped the plate back in front of Jericho, then returned to his plate of pork chops smothered in mushroom gravy, giving Jericho a distracted smile when he'd offered thanks.

Feeling them on either side of him now, supporting him without being obtrusive about it, Jericho let his mind drift back to the memory of what had happened next.

"You don't have to go out of your way for me." Silence met his announcement, and Jericho kept his gaze fixed firmly on the TV, not recognizing the movie that had been playing for the past forty-five minutes.

"Out of our way?" Trent's question hung in the air before he followed it with, "By doing what?"

"I mean—" He felt the flush of hot blood in his cheeks. "By not doin'…whatever. I'm not gonna be offended if y'all hold hands or anything."

Jacob made a sound like he'd tasted something bad, and Jericho wanted to look at him but instead kept his gaze resolutely directed forwards.

Trent shifted around, sitting sideways on the couch towards where Jericho sat on the other end. Jacob had taken the chair earlier, propping his socked feet on the coffee table. From the corner of his eye, Jericho saw a flash of white as they disappeared and heard the squeak of leather as Jacob sat forwards.

"Like, it won't be the end of the world." Jericho cleared his throat. He needed Trent to understand. "If y'all hold hands or somethin'."

"We didn't want to make you uncomfortable." Jacob's words held firm, the truth in them as unmovable as the man seemed to be himself. "I'll admit we've…dialed it back a little."

Jericho shrugged, hoping it looked as if it didn't matter to him. "Undial it if you want."

There was more squeaking of leather; then he felt Jacob's presence standing in front of Trent. On TV, a man and woman ran up a darkened street, either chasing or following…something. An ungodly screech sounded from beside him, and Jericho jerked to the side, twisting to see Jacob had flung himself into Trent's lap and was writhing around, face pressed to the side of Trent's neck, unmistakable sounds of wet raspberries filling the air. The squeal had come from Trent, who was now laughing hysterically, voice rising and falling as it went from words to laughter and back again. "Ohmygodstopit." Laughter. "Jacob Grimes, stop it now." More laughter as Trent tried ineffectually to push Jacob away. "Jakey, pul-ease."

Jacob finally lifted his head and looked at Jericho, then winked. "Thank God I don't have to keep it dialed back." He shifted, sat on the cushion beside Trent, and rested a palm-up hand on his thigh. A moment later, Trent's hand covered Jacob's, and Jericho watched as their fingers fell between each other as if they'd done this a thousand times. "We weren't sure how cool you'd be with even this." He lifted the joined hands, bringing them to his mouth and placing a kiss on the back of Trent's. "With everything—we know it's a lot of change all at once and want you to feel okay about whatever."

"It… You can't change for me." What Jericho didn't say was how terrified he'd already been, concocting scenarios where they quickly became tired of him, of everything, and went back on the offers previously made. "You wouldn't be happy."

Trent leaned forwards and looked at him, then scoffed and sat back. "Huh."

"What?" Jericho bent at the waist and craned his neck until he could see Trent's face. "What's wrong?"

"Nothing." The amusement in Trent's voice gave lie to the word.

"There's somethin'." Jericho squinted. Now Jacob was twisted and looking at Trent. "See? Even Jacob thinks so."

"Jake." Jacob's piercing gaze turned on Jericho. "Family and special friends call me Jake."

"Jake thinks so, too." Warmth built in his chest as he realized they were all teasing each other. "Y'all are crazy."

"Welcome to the club." Trent leaned sideways until his head could tip and touch Jacob's. "What's your middle name, Jericho?"

"Michael." He paused and thought, then asked, "What's yours?"

Trent's lips spread in a wide smile, and he cut his eyes towards Jericho. "Michael."

"Nuh-uh."

"Yeah, huh. Your mom and me, we were peas in a pod for years. Even if she cut me out of your lives, she kept me close, too." Trent's eyes drifted closed, and Jericho was exhausted all of a sudden. "When I left, I missed her most of all."

"Ready?" Jacob, steady and unflappable, waited at his side, hand under Jericho's arm. Trent was on his other side, hand curled tightly around Jericho's.

He nodded, and they began the endless, yet all-too-quickly completed walk to the edge of a yawning hole in the ground. There was a complicated scaffolding across it holding up the casket. When Jericho had blanched at the costs of the coffins, Trent had stepped in and selected exactly what he would have picked out. Glossy wood, brass handles, and the insides were the softest ivory fabric Jericho'd ever felt.

Back at the funeral home for the viewing this morning, his mother had looked pretty lying there in her dress, her grandmother's locket resting in the hollow of her throat. Pretty, but not there, her shell so clearly empty that he felt it was unreal. Like she was a mannequin or something, a prop to take his mother's place, and for an instant, he'd nurtured the fantasy that nothing was real. He'd known the truth, though, and his wishing hadn't stopped the tears from rolling down his face while he stood there, knuckles white as his fingers clenched the edge of the casket. He'd heard Trent murmur something to Jacob, and a moment later, he'd felt them as they were now, bracketing him with their strength.

Trent wavered, and Jericho jerked his arm up, holding tight. "I got you," he whispered into the silence.

"You do, Jericho. You have both of us." Trent's arm went around his shoulder. "I got you back."

The preacher's voice was droning, issuing what Jericho was sure were kind words. There was a pause, and he realized Trent and Jacob were both looking at him, the preacher too, and he grasped that this was the moment they'd talked about earlier. Where if he wanted to say something, he'd be given the chance.

Jericho found he had something to say.

He pushed up from the chair and faced the casket, the drape of white and pink daisies pretty against the warmth of the wood.

"Come here. Come with me." Trent stood as he spoke, then led Jericho towards the end where the preacher had spoken from. Jericho found himself adrift, a tiny sea of concerned faces aimed at him.

With a deep breath in, he started, speaking from the heart. "My mom's the best. She does...did whatever was needed to make sure I had enough, that we had enough. I don't want to let what that man did to her be what makes up all my memories of her. He took enough of her from me. He doesn't get to take this. My mom told me to be kind, to help our neighbors. She taught me that beauty isn't the same for everyone. Once, she told me that it was a sin how folks kept their best opinions of people until they were dead. So I promised her I wouldn't do that, and now"—he took a deep breath as he glanced at the coffin, the box that contained what had been the most important part of his world—"at least I don't have to worry that she didn't know how much I loved her. I told her every day. And me? I don't have to wonder, either." He stood straighter, lifted his chin.

"This is the truth as I know it. My mother was Estelle Marie Conway, and she loved me. Her smile was brighter than the stars, and I'm proud to be her son."

There was shuffling from the people in the chairs, and a single irreverent clap that nearly tore laughter from his throat. Then Trent's arms were around him and Jericho was holding on, tighter and tighter because suddenly he was drowning in grief and pain, and a sobbing rat-a-tat ripped free with raw sounds. Voices spoke out, and he heard the preacher's final words as they stood beside him. And it was done.

Jericho lifted his head to see the mourners straggling off, making their way down the hill and to the cars parked in the lanes threading through the cemetery. Except for a persistent group standing nearer the tent. Jacob stood and looked around, and Jericho saw recognition on his face, a smile that broke through the shared pain like a laser as he called out, "James."

Trent tensed, then relaxed, and he murmured for Jericho's benefit, "Jakey's sister, Jaime. I didn't think they were able to come. It's good, Jericho. It's fine. That's her and her husband, Connor, and their boys Nate and Matt. Matt's the little one."

Jericho swiped at his eyes with his hand, blinking against the tears. He saw a pretty woman wrap her arms around Jacob, stretching to her toes to press a kiss against his cheek. Jacob released her, touched his lips to the top of her head, then was engulfed in a hug from the man who also brushed a kiss against Jacob's cheek. The two boys stood close, the younger already reaching with his hands in a demanding "pick me up" gesture.

"Come on, I'll introduce you." Trent grabbed Jericho's hand and had him moving before he knew what was going on. "Jaime, gorgeous, just look at you. You're absolutely glowing, darling." He wrapped an arm around Jericho's shoulders. "This is my nephew, Jericho."

Jaime stepped closer, her gaze on his face as she said, "I'm so sorry to hear what happened." Her eyes turned to Trent, and she offered her cheek for his kiss. "You know I always love any chance to see you guys, but I truly hate the reason. I'm so sorry, Trent." Behind her, Connor had finally released Jacob, who'd crouched down to talk to Nate, little Matt wedging his way in between them, arms around Jacob's neck.

Trent's voice was soft when he responded. "Thank you, beautiful girl. When did you get in? Just now?"

"No, we made it, barely. Only Con could have turned what should have been a five-hour drive into seven."

"Seven? That seems unlikely."

"We came by way of Chattanooga."

"Ah."

There were sounds from the rise behind them, and Jericho stepped away from Trent to turn and look. Three men clustered around the casket. The conversations behind him faded, muting and becoming muffled, as if they were happening yards away instead of feet. He watched as the men began to turn and twist handles they'd fitted to the scaffolding. It took a second before he realized what they were doing, the coffin slowly lowering into the ground.

Heartbeat pounding in his ears, he found himself unable to look away. The daisies were almost even with the ground when Trent's arm pulled him sideways until he collided with him. There was silence in the cemetery now, all conversations stopped, and he glanced to the side to see Jacob next to Trent, their hands clasped tightly together. Next to him was Jaime—holding Jacob's other hand—and her two sons, then the man, Connor. When Jericho looked back at the gravesite, all that was left were the three men still working the cranks, but even that activity only lasted for another minute before it was done. When the men straightened, one of them glanced around and saw the group staring at him. "Sorry," he called out. "We thought y'all were leavin'."

"Jericho, do you want to stay and watch?"

He shook his head, unable to tear his gaze away from the men as they disassembled the mechanism, quiet clanks of metal on metal as the poles and struts were laid into a wheelbarrow parked nearby. One of the men fiddled with something on the ground and then flipped back a piece of green fabric so Jericho could see the raw earth underneath. It looked stark, like an unhealed scar against otherwise pristine skin.

"Come on, then." The arm around his shoulder urged him to turn, and he did, but he twisted his neck to keep watching. All the way down the hill, he stumbled and swayed as toes and heels tripped and sank into unseen holes. Each of the men had a shovel in hand and was bent to his work, an easy rhythm to their movements. Stoop, scoop, twist, and fling. They were far enough away he couldn't hear the sound the dirt made as it hit the wooden casket.

He was glad of that.

Voices and hands urged him into the car, and through the tinted glass, he watched, turning to look out the rear window as they drove away until he couldn't pick out the men's outlines from the tree line anymore.

Chapter Five
Trent

"Where's your room?"

Trent had asked the question of Jaime but was watching Jacob as he stood at the minibar, pouring from bottles that were nowhere near mini. When Jacob walked the glasses to the occupants of the room, he did so with one stiff leg, toe of his boot lifted to keep Matt's bottom in place where the boy had latched on to his uncle. Trent lifted his chin as he took the tumbler filled with bourbon, and Jacob obliged, pressing a kiss to his lips. Eyes opened throughout the kiss, Trent was treated to a close-up view of Jacob's face softening, the stress easing with the pleasure of connecting like this.

Jaime was next to Trent on the couch, and he watched with surprise as she turned down the drink, opting instead for, "Just pop or water, Jake, thanks."

He darted his gaze to Connor, seated in the chair, and caught the man looking at his wife with a loving and long-suffering expression. Certain now that he wouldn't be telling tales out of school, he blurted, "You're preggers. Oh. My. God." Her wide-eyed look was the final validation that he'd guessed correctly, and he crowed. "You *are*. Oh my Jesus, that's perfect. Perfection. When were you gonna tell your brudder?" Glancing back at Connor, Trent added, "Good job, big man. No test tubes this time around, am I right?"

Connor laughed aloud as Jaime dropped her chin to her throat, shaking her head back and forth as she laughed. "We are," she confirmed, then laughed softly. "This didn't seem the right time, so I was going to wait to tell you."

"Not around my husband," Jacob said on a chuckle. "Congrats, James. That's amazing."

Trent threaded his arm around her shoulders and pulled her sideways against him. "Tell Uncle Trentie everything this little one needs. We'll have another baby shower. Every child should be celebrated." There were sounds from the other end of the room where the boys were, and he turned to look that direction.

His eyes narrowed when he saw Nate staring at Jericho with a wildly disbelieving expression. When he focused, he could just pick out the words when Nate leaned towards Jericho and said, "You can't quit school. School's the most important thing in your life right now. It's the foundation of everything to come."

Jericho's back was towards the adults, so he couldn't hear him, but Nate's response gave him all the clues he needed to know what was said. "No way. Nope. They'd never think that. They might not have known you long, but they already love you. You don't have to try and pull your weight like that. Was your mom gonna let you quit?"

Jericho's nod broke Trent's heart.

Nate's fierce expression as he swung his head back and forth helped salve that wound a little. "No way that's happening now. Not on my watch." Nate lifted his voice, ignoring the frantic arm-waving Jericho launched into. "Dad, do we still have the money from that grant I got for housing?"

"What, son?" Connor's voice was deep and resonated with love for this boy who wasn't his but was all the more his for that fact.

Jaime had been pregnant when her first love had died in a car crash, and she'd been on her own with Nathan for the first ten years of his life, before their world collided with Connor's. Con had fallen in love not just with Jaime, but her son, and once he'd found what he wanted, he hadn't stopped working until they were a family. Of course, it didn't hurt she'd gifted him with a second son almost nine months to the day from when they met, but that was a different story.

"Nothing, Mr. Thompson." Trent saw the arm-waving had stopped, but the boys' heads were close together, their conversation quiet enough he could no longer tell what was said.

Something to explore with Jericho after Jaime and her crew left for their room. Which brought him full circle.

"Where's your room?"

Jaime laughed, taking a glass of clear, bubbly liquid from Jacob. "We're up a couple of floors. Now let's talk about next week." She sipped and smacked her lips. "Perfect, Jake, thanks. Tomorrow you're in court, and with everything that's happened, you said there shouldn't be any issues, right?"

"Right. The will ties it all up in a tidy package. But it wouldn't matter either way; he's ours now." Trent stated it firmly, lifting his voice slightly just in case Jericho was listening. "Then we've got a couple of days of appointments to finish Stella's estate."

"And then you're coming to our house. I'll invite Con's family over and we'll do a mini-reunion party." Jaime mock scowled at him. "No arguments, either. Jake already told me you guys are driving back and have no timeline, so don't get shifty, buster."

Trent held up a hand as he gave her a smile. "Wouldn't think about it, baby sister. No argument from me."

Later, after Jaime and Con left with their kids, and Jericho had retired to his room with the door closed, they were finally lying in bed, alone. There was just enough light seeping in around the curtains for Trent to make out

Jacob's profile, slow blinks of his lids proof he wasn't able to sleep, either.

"God, the look on that baby's face when he watched his mother be buried." Trent rolled his neck, pressing his cheek tight against Jacob's chest. "Broke my heart."

"Yeah. For me it was at the viewing. I thought he was gonna go down when he first saw her, but he pulled it together. That boy's strong, stronger than I'd be in the same situation." Jacob's voice was tight, filled with emotion. "He's gonna need help, and we're gonna be right there beside him, all the way."

"Did you catch whatever that conversation was he had with Nate?"

Jacob scoffed, chest rising and falling with a deep sigh. "No, but Nate texted me some stuff. He said Jericho's feeling indebted and doesn't like having the scales out of balance. He included a bunch of links for articles on teenaged grief and how kids process differently than adults." His hand landed on Trent's shoulder, fingers tracing up and down the skin of his arm until Trent shivered. "Then he sent me another bunch of links on schools in the Memphis area. My nephew's not-too-subtle attempt to influence us to move back to Memphis."

"He's such a good kid."

"That kid's going to graduate from college next year. At thirteen. So damn smart, but what I'm always impressed with is his heart. You're right, he's a good kid. Con said he's going to have his pick of graduate programs. Guess they're falling all over themselves to get a chance at him." Jacob wrapped his arms around Trent, pulling him close for a moment. "Smart, heart, and got his head on straight. Nate's something else."

"Do you want to move back to Memphis? I know we've talked about it in very broad terms. We even talked about it with Jericho. It's terrifying to think about because we're serious this time." Trent relaxed into Jacob's hold. "I'm not against it because where you go, I go, and that's all I need, but I know the area has bad memories for you."

"It's got good ones, too."

"And your sister."

Under Trent's cheek, Jacob's heart beat steadily, a dependable cadence that was much like Jacob himself.

"And James and her crew. God help us." A chuckle shook Jacob's chest just before his lips pressed to Trent's temple. Trent smiled at the fond exasperation in Jacob's tone. "She's pregnant. I'm so glad for her and Con."

"It's got surrogacy clinics, too. We know that for sure. We can talk to Con's brother and see if they liked the one they went through." Trent's proclamation was met with silence, and he pulled back, narrowing his eyes to focus on Jacob. "Honey?"

"I think...babe, I think that's something we're going to have to put on hold for now." Jacob's eyes were closed, face pointed towards the ceiling, and nothing in his expression gave any indication what he might be thinking.

"You wanted a baby." Trent leaned closer, and fingers trailing through the scruff on Jacob's jaw, he turned Jacob to face him. "We want a baby."

"We've got our nephew now." Jacob looked puzzled. "You just said we were going to be busy helping him deal."

"Well, yeah." Trent paused, working through the best way to say what he was thinking. "But you've been so excited about the whole enchilada. Picking a surrogate, seeing the ultrasounds, being there for the birth. I don't want you to miss out on anything you wanted."

"Trent, it doesn't matter that Jericho's older, that's he's not an infant or even a toddler. He's depending on us to be there for him, to make the right decisions for him, and to love him unconditionally." Jacob turned on his side, facing Trent. "We don't always get to choose who God puts in our path." He pushed up on an elbow and placed a hand on Trent's chest. "He's given us Jericho, and I am thrilled to be provided such a profound chance to father the boy as best I can. It's not about having a child as a baby. For me, it's always been about the opportunity to nurture a being, helping them along and giving them the freedom and space to be the best they can be." Jacob leaned closer, his expression earnest and open. "Jericho's needs don't exclude mine. They're in alignment."

Trent lifted his chin, and Jacob brushed a kiss across his lips.

"Okay." He released the word on a sigh, trying unsuccessfully to deepen the kiss.

Trent felt Jacob's smile as his lips dusted another caress along Trent's mouth, giving an amused shake of his head.

His husband nuzzled the side of his face before pulling back and asking, "Okay? That's it?"

With a shrug, Trent nodded. "Yeah, okay. You said it all, I think." He scowled up at Jacob. "The only thing I wanna know is how can you be so eloquent at times like these, and at other times you *think*"—he made air quotes with the fingers of one hand—"you communicate the same depth of knowledge with a single 'babe'? Huh?"

Jacob's hand slipped underneath the covers, skating along Trent's chest to his briefs. Trent closed his eyes as hot fingertips traced the outline of his rapidly hardening cock through the fabric. Then Jacob chuckled, kissed him through the laughter, and murmured a quiet "Babe" against his lips.

"Oh my Jesus."

Jericho

Sighing, he cracked one eyelid open and peered at the screen of the phone lying on the hotel room nightstand. Just after midnight, and he was still awake. Jericho flopped onto his back, spreading arms and legs out like a starfish. The bed was so big—and comfortable. Too much so.

The phone was still a novelty, something he wasn't yet accustomed to, a gift from Jake. *And Trent*, he supposed, but it had been Jake who'd disappeared for a time yesterday, coming back with the newest version of a popular model. He'd spent a half hour showing Jericho how to work it, setting his and Trent's numbers up as favorites.

Nate had entered his number in, too, taking the device from Jericho and handling it deftly. The years separating them felt like they went the wrong way, with Nate seeming to have so much more experience in everything. He'd never met a smarter kid. The boy was in college for Christ's sake, and talking to Nate was like having a conversation with an adult. How he looked at things was so matter-of-fact, with everything he said coming out sounding like truth.

Even when Jericho disagreed with him.

He knew he had to contribute. It was not only how he'd been raised, but Jericho had never had anything worth losing before, nothing that mattered as much as making certain Trent and Jake didn't get tired of having him around.

Still, if Nate was right and they wouldn't let him quit school to find a job, he'd have to sort out some other way to make himself not only useful, but indispensable.

Because the other things Nate had told him made Jericho understand how fragile his existence with Trent and Jake was.

They wanted a baby. Had been working to have one through a clinic in California, so they could adopt.

But now they'd been saddled with Jericho instead.

He rolled to his side, curling his knees towards his chest as he tugged the covers up and over his head, creating a darkened cocoon. He shivered, limbs trembling despite the warmth encircling him.

Why would she keep her own brother a secret?

Even without asking himself the question, he knew. His mom might have looked sad when Frank was berating Jericho for his shortcomings as a stepson, but the only time she'd left the room was when Frank started in on him about being a pervert. Calling him a deviant, talking about Sodom and pillars of bitter salt, about sins of the flesh, sins against God, giving in to the devil—Frank had a thousand sayings, each accompanied by his belt or his fist.

It made sense now, because her own brother was gay.

No wonder she hadn't bothered defending Jericho.

His chest hitched, and he pushed his face against the pillow.

She hated gays. Hated Trent.

Throat burning, lungs aching for air, Jericho struggled to keep his grief silent.

Probably hated me.

The door clicked and he froze, holding in place, not wanting anyone to see him this vulnerable. His body had other ideas, though, and a sob broke free, loud and echoing under the covers.

"Oh, honey." Trent's voice was soft and quiet. "You can't sleep either?" The bed depressed beside him, covers tightening around Jericho as Trent curled up against his back, surrounding him protectively. Jericho's good hand gripped the blankets when Trent pulled on them, keeping them overhead. "Okay, then. You stay like that." Strong arms surrounded him, comforting arms, and Jericho marveled at how he understood in his gut that Trent would protect him against the world. "I've got you, baby boy. I've got you."

The tears flowed, and with burning eyes, Jericho sucked in great gasps of air between sobs, face wet with salt and sweat. He didn't speak, didn't have to, because Trent had lost someone, too. He understood.

It took a long time, but his grief finally waned, ebbing away slowly. Through it all, Trent had kept up a quiet patter of supportive words. Never demanding an answer, not even urging Jericho to stop taking up so much of his time—just being there.

"I'm sorry." It took three tries, but Jericho finally got his apology out.

"Nothing to be sorry about, baby boy." Trent's fingers cupped Jericho's shoulder through the blankets, squeezed, then released. "It's gonna happen sometimes. Something I've learned is when a feeling that strong takes hold, we've just got to ride it out. I'm just glad I was here to ride it out with you."

Stifled suddenly by the heat captured by the blankets, Jericho yanked them down, taking in great lungsful of cool air, his wet skin prickling in the unexpected chill. Trent's fingers pushed through his hair, and Jericho turned to face him, leaning in as Trent pulled him close. He was braver in the dark, just like back in the hospital, so he blurted his worst secret. "I'm gay."

♥ ♥ ♥

Trent

Oh, Lord.

Trent froze at Jericho's admission, something he'd suspected, and Jacob had confirmed he had his own belief of the same. With a quiet sigh, Trent forced his hand to keep moving, fingers threading through Jericho's sweat-clumped hair. If this was what he thought, then he might be the first person Jericho had willingly come out to, and he was terrified of screwing things up.

"Did you hear me?" Jericho's voice cracked, wavering on the question, a demand that he be heard, that Trent acknowledge his statement.

"I heard you." Trent tightened his arm around Jericho when the boy would have pushed off, the heavy cast wedged between them. Then he told him everything Trent wished he'd heard from family and friends when he'd made the same declaration, so many years ago. Nothing about religion, nothing about it being a phase, and nothing about it being an obvious trait. This was Jericho's news to share, and Trent wanted him to know how honored he felt. "I heard you, baby boy. I heard you, and I believe you. Thank you for trusting me with this. It has to be hard to tell someone you didn't know existed even a week ago, so thank you."

Silence greeted his words. Then Jericho's body jerked with a suppressed sob.

"You believe me?"

"Yeah, of course I do. The world isn't always kind to people who identify outside what society determines is the norm. There's no reason for a body to borrow that kind of grief, unless it was true." Trent's mouth filled with bitter saliva. "I know, baby boy. I truly know."

"Momma hated it."

He let that statement hang in the air, waiting, because there had to be more. Jericho finally followed up with what he'd been avoiding saying before.

"I think she hated me a little bit, too."

The only response Trent could think of was to hold Jericho a little tighter. His sister had kept Jericho a secret from him, so he couldn't honestly acknowledge or deny Jericho's words. He knew what he hoped his sister would have done, loving her only child no matter what. But the stark reality of his own coming out stripped those beliefs thin.

"Did she hate you? Is that why she never told me about you? You're family. If she could do that to you, then…"

This, Trent knew how to answer, even if it was with just his desperate hope. "Jericho, your mother loved you. The way she stood up to Frank that day, following through with the police? That's not the act of a woman who doesn't love her child. She loved you, and that's all you need to know. There's no good going to come out of wondering what if, and baby boy, every one of us needs all the good we can get in life. She loved you. Full stop. Hold tight to that, because it is true."

They stayed like that for long minutes, the only sound their respirations, Trent's slow and even, Jericho's quick, distressed at first before finally settling into the same rhythm as Trent's.

Then Jericho's stomach complained, a long, rumbling growl that was loud in the quiet.

Trent held his breath until Jericho giggled. Then it was on, their unexpected laughter growing, swelling, bleeding off tension in healthy ways, continuing until Jacob's voice came from the doorway.

"What's so funny?"

Trent looked over to see Jacob knuckling at his eyes like a child, hair mussed, tight tee showing off his muscles, sleep shorts hanging off his hips.

"Hey, honey." Trent made to sit up, pausing when Jericho's hand clenched tight around his. "I think Jericho's hungry. His stomach sounds like it's about to come out and attack us if we don't feed him, STAT."

"I'm not sure what's in the kitchen, but I bet we can rustle something up." Jacob turned to walk away with a smile. "Come on out when you're ready."

Jericho's stomach grumbled again, and Trent was the first to laugh this time. "Let's go, kiddo." He rolled off the mattress and to his feet, turning to see Jericho sitting in the middle of the bed, covers puddled around him. "You coming?"

"Yeah." Jericho shook his head. "Just…you guys are awesome."

"We try," Jacob called from farther out in the suite.

"Honey," Trent chastised, grinning because he knew what was coming next.

"Babe."

He glanced back at Jericho and rolled his eyes, earning a tiny giggle.

They were clustered around the tiny kitchenette, Trent watching as Jacob put another pair of bread slices into the toaster. He'd commandeered the whole process, declaring it a single-man job, and was busily scraping tiny pads of butter onto the most recently retrieved slices.

Jericho was standing next to Trent, crowding him a little. Fidgeting with the hem of his shirt, Jericho wasn't looking at either of them as he shuffled his weight from foot to foot. Trent bumped Jericho's shoulder with his, catching a glimpse of the boy's anguished expression.

"I'm gay." Much as they had earlier, the blurted words came as a surprise, and Trent jerked his full gaze over to the boy. Jericho seemed to be intently studying his toes, scrunching and unscrunching them against the cold tile floor.

"Yeah?" Jacob half turned, tossing a glance over his shoulder at the boy, then to Trent. "Cool." He turned back to the toast, placing it on the small tower of already prepared slices stacked on a plate. "Is there any jelly at all?"

"That's all? Cool?" Jericho's mouth hung open, eyes wide in surprise. "You aren't mad at me or anything?"

"Mad?" Jacob sounded faintly puzzled, the line of his shoulders relaxed and easy. "You do something wrong?"

"Well, I'm gay." Now Jericho's chin was up, and he leaned forwards slightly.

"Jesus, kid." Jacob turned, one corner of his mouth lifting in that way Trent loved. "So am I. Why the hell would I be pissed you're gay?"

"I don't know, maybe because I didn't tell you earlier?"

"Are you looking for a fight for some reason?" Jacob lifted the plate of buttered toast and held the food at arm's length to Jericho. "I think you're hangry. Have a slice on me."

Jericho turned his gaze on Trent, accusation in every line of his tense body. "Did you tell him?"

"No, kiddo. What you choose to share, or not share, that's all on you. I'm the last person who'd want to out someone, not even if I believed the person I'd be including in your secret would be supportive." Trent shook his head. "Not happening."

"Oh." Jericho appeared to deflate slightly. "I'm sorry, Jacob. I'm not sure what's wrong with me."

"Jake," Jacob promptly reminded him, and smiled broadly when Jericho nodded. "Right now I'm not going to read too much into anything you do that seems off. You've been through a lot in a little time, and our job here is to help you come out the other end as whole as we can manage." He shoved the plate into Jericho's hands just as the toaster popped out the next slices. "Now eat, before your stomach starts in on your backbone."

A bemused-looking Jericho turned and wandered to the couch, settling on the floor with the plate on the coffee table in front of him. He used the remote to click on the TV and immediately went to the menu, scrolling through the offerings until he found something that interested him.

With the soft sounds from the TV as background noise, Trent made his way to Jacob and fit himself against his husband's back, wrapping his arms around Jacob's waist.

"So he outed himself to you, huh?" Jacob's voice was low and quiet. Trent nodded against his back, forehead pressed tight to Jacob's spine. "Not unexpected, but why now?"

"I woke up to him crying." That was all Trent had to say; he felt Jacob's muscles tense everywhere they touched.

"His mom." The pain in Jacob's voice echoed the emotions Trent had struggled through earlier as he tried to comfort Jericho. *I love him so much.* His husband was a good man.

"Yeah. And all the what-ifs that come along with why she didn't tell him they weren't alone."

"Fuck." Jacob cursed softly, head swinging slowly back and forth in denial.

"Yeah."

"And he came out to you." Jacob's gentle jostling movements as he buttered the toast rocked Trent against his back. "Not like we didn't already know."

"Yeah, but to say it straight out like that takes courage." Trent sighed and gave Jacob a squeeze before releasing him and turning, propping a hip against the counter. "How do we help him through this? I know what I had hoped for when I was forced out of the closet, but what did I know? This poor kiddo has lost so very much, and then to take on something like coming out on top of it. I just want to do right by him."

"He picked a good person and the right time, but 3:00 a.m. courage only goes so far." Jacob lifted a piece of toast and held it while Trent took a bite. "You're good for him. You got this, babe."

Trent stared at Jericho's silhouette, framed against the flashing colors of some anime show. He chewed slowly, then swallowed, throat tight.

"I hope so, Jakey. I truly hope so."

Chapter Six

Trent

"Did you check the bathroom?" One hand placed flat on top of his suitcase, Trent shoved hard as he tried to zip it closed, fingers of his other hand alternating between tugging the zipper tab and tucking the folds and corners of every article of clothing determined to escape confinement. "And the kitchenette thingie?"

Jacob's arm went around his waist, one palm landing beside his on the suitcase and pressing down firmly. "Yes, and yes."

With two hands to tackle the actual fastening process, Trent made better headway. "Did you check the drawers in the dressers? How about the couch cushions? The bathroom?" He tugged the tab around the final corner of the suitcase and sighed heavily. "There. Done."

Straightening, he looked at Jacob and didn't understand the broad grin on his face. "What?"

"Babe." Jacob pushed in for a kiss, and Trent happily obliged, eyes dipping closed as their lips connected in a quick brushing caress. When Jacob pulled back, he yanked on the suitcase, letting the luggage slip over the edge of the bed as he extended the handle. Without another word, he turned to walk out of the hotel bedroom, and Trent stared after him.

"That's not a whole conversation, Jakey." He glanced around the room, moving to the nearby nightstand to pull open the drawer, finding it empty.

"Babe."

At Jacob's one-word repeated rejoinder, Trent let his head drop back and asked the ceiling, "Does the man ever answer my questions? No. No he does not."

"Yeah, I do. And I did." Jacob's voice was louder, and when Trent turned, he found him standing in the doorway. "Yes, I checked the bathroom twice. And the dresser. And the closet, even though you haven't asked about that yet. We didn't put anything in the nightstands, so I'm not sure what you expect to find except for religious propaganda. We're ready, Trent. Let's hit the road."

"Is Jericho ready? Does he need help packing? Is the suitcase we got him big enough for everything?" Trent walked towards Jacob, expecting him to move out of the way, and was drawn up short when the man stood firm against his determined approach. "Let me by, sweetheart. I want to help Jericho."

"Trent." When that was all that was forthcoming, Trent bugged his eyes out with lifted brows. His waiting was finally rewarded by a soft touch against his cheek. "He's good. Suitcase is good. Everything's good. Stop. Freaking. Out." The last three words were interrupted with quick pecking kisses, ending with a loud smack that made him smile. "You good?"

The pressure that had been coiling inside his chest like an overwound spring slowly relaxed, and Trent took in a shaky breath as he nodded. "I don't know what's wrong with me. It's just a little court appearance and then we're on the road."

"It's them giving Jericho to us, the first step on making it permanently official. I think I'd be disappointed if it didn't freak you out a little, but babe." Jacob kissed him again, slipping his tongue between Trent's lips and drawing a soft moan from him. Their foreheads pressed together, and when Trent's eyes slowly opened, he found Jacob staring at him. "Trentie, this is over the top, even for you."

He pulled back, pretending to be offended. "Hey. Not funny."

"It's a little bit funny." Jacob's hand fumbled against his, and their fingers fell together. "You gotta admit it's a little funny."

"I admit nothing." Arm around Jacob's neck, he drew himself down for another kiss. "Except the fact that I love you deliriously."

Jacob stepped back and to the side, pulling Trent forwards. "Let's blow this popsicle stand."

"You can blow me." Trent thought he'd kept his suggestion quiet, but a loud *ewwww* from the couch made him grin. "Sorry," he called, grinning too wide for his apology to Jericho to be authentic. "Good habits die hard."

"You make me hard," Jacob muttered, and Trent laughed.

"Dad jokes." He lifted his voice an octave and, adding an extra level of sashay to his walk, trilled out a hyper enthusiastic, "Lov*e* it!"

Jericho was watching them closely from where he sat on the arm of the couch. He had an overstuffed duffel at his feet next to the large suitcase they'd bought for him. Still, it made Trent's heart hurt to know what was in those two pieces of luggage represented everything his nephew owned in the world. Over the past two days, they'd gone through the rental house, donating all of Stella's and Frank's clothing to the local charity organizations, doing the same with the mismatched dishes, pots, and pans in the kitchen. Jacob had hauled a small dumpster's worth of trash bags to the end of the driveway, working quietly and efficiently as Trent had followed Jericho through the house, helping the boy make sense of the few things he wanted to keep. It hadn't been much, and that had broken his heart, too.

If only Stella had told him how things were for her, he would have turned over every stone in an attempt to make her and Jericho's lives better. But she hadn't, and there he'd been, sorting through picture after picture in a jumbled box, mapping the outline of their existence. At Jericho's birthday parties in the kitchen of whatever house they'd been inhabiting at the time, the only constant was smiling images of Stella and the boy. He knew even those smiles would haunt him, because neither were free and easy. Both had a tightness he'd remembered from his childhood, tension and fear slipping into too many of the images, especially the earlier ones where his parents were present, too.

Whispering to Jacob last night in the darkness of their bed, he'd mused on how different his and Stella's lives were.

"As tough as it was to start out the way I did, maybe I didn't get the short stick I always thought I had. Jakey, I think her lot in life was ten times worse than I expected. I wish I could have saved her, too."

"Babe." Jacob tightened his arms around Trent, pulling him a little closer. "You were nothing more than a kid; it's a miracle you were able to save yourself. When I think about all the things that could have happened to you." Jacob's voice trembled and broke, and his lips were soft against Trent's temple as he pressed a tender kiss there. When he continued talking, his tone was gentle, belying the brutality

of his words. "She was your older sister. Older, and from what you've shared, she was both smart and capable, and she still didn't step up for you. Babe, she knew what your parents were capable of, but she still subjected her child to them. What do you think she'd have done if your parents hadn't passed away and Jericho was questioning his sexuality? She should have been your protector and wasn't. Would she have been his? I don't think people deserve bad things to happen, but when you left, she could have saved herself and didn't. You can't take that on, and I won't let you."

"She was just a kid, too, Jakey. It's not like either of us knew what we were doing." He rolled his head and dropped a kiss against Jacob's chest. "I wish I'd been there for her with the baby, and then after Jericho was born." They lay in silence for a moment; then Trent whispered, "I don't think she'd have given him my middle name if she hated me." Tears welled in his eyes, and he tried to ignore them, hoping they'd dry up and just go away. He'd cried so much over the past week, every nerve felt raw and flayed. "Do you think she hated me?"

"No, doll. I don't. I don't think that." Jacob rolled them so Trent faced him across a handspan of smooth pillow. He knew the tears hadn't disappeared when Jacob groaned and pulled him close, letting Trent bury his face in Jacob's neck. "Don't cry, baby. Don't cry. She didn't hate you. She couldn't have. She left you Jericho, the most precious thing in her world. That's not the action of a woman who hated you. She loved you. You love her, and she loved you. Named her baby boy after her baby brother, to keep a little bit of

you alive in her world, no matter she wasn't strong enough to bring you back. She loved you, I promise."

Trent's eyes stung now with the remembered tears he'd shed as Jacob held him, keeping up the continuous stream of comforting words that eventually had worked their magic, letting him drift off to sleep with only good dreams about his husband and Jericho.

Blinking fiercely, he forced a smile on his face, letting it stay in place until the expression felt more comfortable and real, then clapped his hands together and waved at the door. "Let's get this show on the road, my friends. Time to roll."

They'd upgraded the rental to an SUV, looking for more comfort as they made the long road trip to California via Memphis, and once the luggage was stored in the cargo area, they made the short drive to the courthouse. As nervous as Trent had felt about it, the actual hearing took less than five minutes, that single piece of paper written in Stella's precise penmanship making all the difference. Trent had glanced back at the doors with tears in his eyes, ready to escape the stuffy room and tell his guys it was official. Two signatures later, he did just that, and the way Jericho's face lit up when Trent waved the folder at them made his heart soar.

Trent directed Jacob to a local grocery store to load up on snacks. The inside was startlingly familiar, low shelves allowing customers to help themselves, and the fruit, dairy, and meat sections were in exactly the same place they'd been when he was last here so many years ago.

Jericho was quiet as they walked through the store. With Trent's constant pestering, he finally selected various junk food options and threw them into the basket Jacob carried. At the checkout stands was the first place Jericho spoke up, his face suddenly animated and almost frantic as he directed them into a particular line. After Trent noticed it was longer than the one at the only other open register in the store, he realized Jericho hadn't been herding them to a line so much as away from the other one.

Studying the other cashier from the corner of his eye, he saw the young man kept glancing at Jericho—who was doing a terrible job of ignoring him, casting the same covert looks back at the boy. Trent took a step closer to Jericho, leaning into his side to whisper, "Who's the handsome hunka-hunka who can't keep his eyes off you?"

"What?" Jericho jerked away, cheeks flaming pink. "That's not—no he's not."

"Oh, yes." Lips pursed to keep from grinning wide, Trent nodded fast but kept his voice quiet. "Mmhmm. He so is." Jericho's eyes widened, and he looked panicked. Trent decided to involve his better half and leaned the other way, resting his cheek on Jacob's shoulder as he whispered, "Jakey, did you see the cutie on lane four?"

"See what, babe?" Jacob turned away from the magazine rack he'd been looking at and glanced around, quickly homing in on the other cashier, too. "Oh, he's a pretty one." He turned to face Jericho and dipped his head when he asked, "You know him?"

"Uh, that's Marco." Jericho's eyes slipped to the side as he looked at the boy again. "He's in my grade."

"He's cute. Did you see his ass? If I didn't have my own hunky husband and he was ten years older, I'd think about tapping that." Jacob angled back towards the magazines, pointing at one with an exceptionally gaudy cover. "You think there's really a bigfoot living outside Seattle?"

"What?" Jericho's voice had gained a higher pitch than Trent had heard it before, and he grinned at Jacob's effective normalizing of their appraisal of another male. Something Jericho clearly had no experience with. "You'd...what?"

"Bigfoot? You think it's real or no?" Their cashier finished scanning everything, and Jacob pulled his wallet out and swiped his card through the machine as Trent moved to bag their purchases. "I'm leaning towards real, because I like to think there's things out there we just haven't earned the right to know about yet." Jericho was suspiciously quiet through the rest of the exchange, and Trent wasn't surprised to see the boy was deep in thought.

As they walked past the other register, Marco called out, "Hey, Jerry, sorry about your mom. Are you okay?"

Jericho's head had dropped even farther between his shoulders as he mumbled a response, but it whipped up as Trent stopped and turned to face the boy.

That name.

Back in the hospital, under the influence of potent painkillers, Jericho had shared it was something Frank had caused, drunkenly declaring Jericho was a fancy name for a fancy boy. Stella's response was to immediately start calling him Jerry instead, trying to keep things on an even keel, but Jericho had hated it. Trent found he wanted to make a statement, but he knew he needed to try and do it without humiliating his nephew.

"Je*richo* will heal and survive, thank you for those sweet words, Marco." Hand on one hip, Trent pulled a tiny layer of flamboyance out of hiding, just enough that if the boy was curious, he'd likely recognize it. With a slinky one-shoulder shrug, he added, "Sorry you're losing him to the lure of California. San Diego has *so* much to offer, we just *have* to take him back with us. You decide you want to *come out*, give Jericho a little ringy-ding." He twirled to face Jacob and Jericho, laughing at their very different expressions. Jacob's was affectionately amused, and Jericho was clearly scandalized. "Ta, Marco." Trent looped his arm through Jacob's and grabbed Jericho's hand, leading them from the store.

They were on the highway before Jericho said anything, and when he did, it wasn't what Trent expected.

"Is that really a thing? Just like...looking at someone?"

"Looking's free. It's never good to embarrass a person, but there's no law against looking, Jericho." Jacob's response was quick and easy, his competent control of the car not changing. "Plus, that boy had a fine ass."

"He really did, didn't he?" Trent threw that comment in before Jericho could respond, and Jacob's eyes sparkled as he glanced Trent's way. "Bubble butt like that, you know that boy's doing his squats."

"Marco's not...like that."

"Oh, I wouldn't be too sure about that." Jacob answered before Trent could once again, and the laughter in his voice made Trent grin. "There's a mirror above the door, and I caught him checking out not just your ass, but the sassy man sitting here next to me, too."

"So that's a thing?"

"Yeah, Jericho." Trent reached over and gripped Jacob's hand, twining their fingers together. "It's a thing." He stifled a laugh. "Did you see his face when I offered to help him come out? He caught the reference, no doubt. I think your crush is crushing on you, too, Jericho."

"What? I'm not—that's not what—" Jericho stopped trying to force his words out for a moment, and his tone was more serious when he asked, "How do people do this?"

"It's easier when I'm with him." Trent tipped his head towards Jacob. "Or with people I trust. And knowing when and where to be open is a skill that we all learn out of self-preservation. That's an unfortunate truth. I won't ever pretend to be something I'm not, but just like we did in the hospital, there's a time and a place."

"Marco's face." Jericho sucked in a deep breath, then surprised Trent by laughing softly. "You might be right."

"Yeah, I might be." Trent turned to look out the side window. "There's a first time for everything."

"Jericho, was there anywhere you wanted to drive past before we leave town?"

Trent smiled at the passing scenery, loving Jacob just a little more for his thoughtful offer. In the side mirror, he could see a blurry outline of Jericho's face as he stared out the window. The movement meant Jericho's headshake preceded his quiet "No," by a few moments, and as much as Jacob's kindness had lifted up Trent only a second ago, the pain in Jericho's ragged voice dragged him to the edge of tears again.

"Okay. Anything you need, just let me know." Jacob once again set the mark for normalizing things, acknowledging Jericho's response without drawing attention to the tears clogging the boy's throat.

"I love you, Jakey." Trent closed his eyes as Jacob's grip on his fingers tightened and relaxed, a sweet squeeze that communicated more than any verbal response would have. He sniffed, blinked, and leaned his head against the back of the seat, hoping both of the people in the car ignored the false note in his enthusiastic cheer. "On to Memphis."

Jericho

About three hours into the drive to Memphis, Jericho unbuckled his seat belt and leaned up between the front seats, glaring at Trent for a moment before he turned and hissed at Jake, "Can I wake him up yet?" The racketing hitch in the continuous snores at his words seemed to underscore the request, and he stared hard at Jake, losing his patience when a response wasn't immediately forthcoming. "Well? I can poke him with the cast just a little and wake him up. He'd never know anything."

"No, leave him." Jake's voice vibrated with laughter, and Jericho didn't miss the fond smile that Jake aimed through the windshield, knowing it was actually directed at Trent. Their love wasn't something they felt the need to talk about constantly, but the demonstration factor was way up there. He'd never seen even one of his mom's boyfriends or her husband treat her with the same kind of steady consideration or look at her the way he'd seen Jake and Trent do with each other often. Jake glanced at Jericho over his shoulder, and for a moment, the beam of his affection was directed Jericho's way, making his chest hurt. Jake's attention wasn't creepy in any way, more of how he thought a favorite uncle would be. *If Trent's my uncle, does that make Jake my uncle, too?* Jake had said as much once, when first talking about Jaime and her family. Jericho didn't have a chance to pursue that thought, because Jake said casually, "He hasn't slept well since we left home."

The reminder that they'd dropped everything to come to his rescue—and the reason why they'd had to make such drastic changes in their schedules—deflated Jericho, and he dropped his chin and muttered, "Right," before he slumped back in his seat, fingers fumbling awkwardly to buckle the seat belt.

He'd overheard Trent on the phone yesterday, soothing clients whose work had been delayed because of what he'd called a personal emergency. Trent had even offered one caller what had to be a steep discount, because he'd winced as he'd said the number, wrinkling his nose when he'd followed up with forced pleasure at the clear acceptance of the concession. Jake's work calls had been different, but similar. He'd been a lot more matter-of-fact about the shifting of deadlines and ended each call with a gruffly spoken thanks to the people on the other end.

They're losing money because of me. Jericho had scarcely slept last night, trying to add up what the trip had cost them so far. Airfare, hotel, car rental, clothing for him—it was a mounting debt he didn't know how he'd be able to repay. Nate's naïve expectation that they didn't want anything in return had derailed some of Jericho's initial plans, but once they got to San Diego, he'd figure out something.

First would be Memphis, though, and Jericho found himself eager to see Nate again. The boy had been fascinating to talk to, and having that differing perspective would not hurt when Jericho was trying to make decisions. He'd just have to keep the boy from telling their uncles about whatever Jericho decided. Surprisingly, Nate seemed to vary from all the stereotypes Jericho had ever seen about the boy wonder geniuses, because he was as far from gullible or immature as he could be. Nate had alluded to things in his background not being the easiest, and that might play into how old he acted. Jericho knew the life his mom and he had lived had made him grow up fast. That had been a constant refrain for her, how she regretted the way circumstances required she lean on Jericho so much.

He stared out the window, gaze skipping along the fences and fields, watching as shadows from clouds raced up to and engulfed whole structures, changing things from bright and cheerful to gloomy in an instant. *I never minded having to step up*. His sore lip complained at how his teeth were abusing it, and he ran his tongue along the swollen flesh. He had minded. Minded doing without. Minded walking into the food bank where his classmates were working alongside their parents, the dynamic shift of power making life hard in and out of school. He'd minded Frank having money for whatever he wanted but his mom not having the cash to buy a new pair of shoes when her old ones got too raggedy to wear.

The horses had been Jericho's idea, the large barn having stood empty for months after they moved into the house. He'd started cleaning it out, repairing things as best he could, begging and borrowing tools and materials from neighbors and other people he knew in town. When he'd approached his mom with his plan, she'd stared at him for a moment then pulled his head against her chest, wrapping her arms around him with a tear-filled mutter. "My boy, always lookin' out for his momma."

I tried.

The memory of Frank that last night tried to surface, wedging itself into his throat and cutting off his air. His tongue felt too large for his mouth as he bit down on his lip to silence the shout of warning he wished he'd been able to give his mom.

The hours he'd spent in the barn, bringing in a small but steady income for them, had been a source of pride for him. That had been Jericho making a difference, stepping up and helping support his mom. Now, the idea that it was what killed her was something he couldn't get away from. No ducking the knowledge that was where she'd died. Where Frank had made a stand with Jericho. Breaking his arm the first in a tragic cascade of events that led to him sitting here, in the back seat of this car, staring out at farms and neighborhoods filled with people going on about their business. He couldn't wrap his head around the fact that none of them, not a single one, knew what had happened to his mom.

Jake appeared in front of the window, and Jericho cried out, cringing back into the seat as the door opened. He hadn't even realized they'd stopped in a rest area, having pulled off the highway and parked in a secluded spot near the end of the lot. Jake squatted down, one hand gripping the armrest molded into the door. His other was raised, with a wad of tissues in it.

Jericho's eyes were burning, watering, tearing up, and overflowing. He reached out with his good hand and took the tissues, dabbing at his face. As tight as his skin felt, eyelids swollen, he'd clearly been crying for a while without even noticing. "Sorry." Fighting the overwhelming need to weep, he clamped his lips together, eyes squeezed closed as he angled his face down. Not so much a desire to hide, because this wasn't the first time Jake had seen him cry, but it always left him feeling vulnerable.

"Come on." He looked up just as Jake leaned over him and unbuckled the seat belt, scooting out of the way to let Jericho climb out of the car. Jake pointed to a nearby picnic table. "Let's sit there for a bit and talk." Jericho followed him up the walkway and climbed up to sit on the tabletop next to Jake, who smiled. "We'll let Trent sleep a little longer."

He took in a big breath, hating the way his shoulders hitched in the middle. "Sorry," he repeated, knowing it was a lousy apology for interrupting their trip like this.

"No sorries, Jericho. You can't bottle feelings like this up. When my sister lost her fiancé, I sat with her for two months straight, every night, so she wouldn't be alone when she was hurting. The pain of losing someone doesn't just go away because we want it to, and the grief of change can be nearly as overwhelming." Jake's voice was quiet, soothing, loud enough to hear over the hum of passing cars and trucks without shouting down the parking lot. "When I lost my parents, because that's how it felt to me when they kicked me out, I was without purpose for weeks. I couldn't imagine someone I loved so much not loving me enough to accept who I was inside. Finding out I'd been wrong, that my trust in my family wasn't deserved, that was grief, too. My friends, their families, all the people I'd known all my life became suspect. Jaime was the only one I believed when she said it didn't matter. Even then, I tested her when I introduced her to your uncle. I told her I was bringing a date, didn't say who, just showed up with my boyfriend—

and not only was she cool with it, she quickly won him over. With his experience, and then hearing about mine, let's just say your uncle wasn't quick to trust."

"Should I call him uncle? You think he'd like that?" Jericho blinked, then cut a glance over to Jake in time to see a bright smile cross his face.

"Yeah, I think he'd like that a lot. He's gutted he didn't get to know you before now, didn't have a place in your life. I think calling him Uncle Trent will go a long way to him believing you don't hate him for not being there."

"Why would I hate him for that? If Mom didn't tell him, then how could he have known?" Jericho straightened and tried not to glare at the idea of Trent thinking something like that. "I don't hate him. Not at all. He's cool. You're both cool."

"Yeah, he's the coolest." They sat in silence for a moment, then Jake asked, "What was your mom like?"

"Oh, man. She was…everything. Didn't matter what happened, she'd find a bright side to it. When it was just her and me, she made everything an adventure." He thought back over all the times they'd been struggling. "She was always smiling. Wasn't a thing in this world that mattered to her more than family." He realized how that sounded and tried to backpedal, glad Trent wasn't there to have heard what he'd just said. "After Mama and Papa died, she made a point to say me and her were going to be okay. I hadn't even thought that we wouldn't be, but she told me she'd learned from someone a long time ago how to be stronger than what life threw at her, and we'd be okay. I think...I think she was talking about Uncle Trent."

"I think she was, too." Jake's head moved in Jericho's peripheral vision, nodding. "Your uncle is one of the strongest men I know."

"Mom was...Jake, I don't know why she picked a man like Frank. I overheard one of her friends telling her she could do better than Frank, and she dropped that friend like a hot potato." He swallowed hard; this felt like telling secrets that weren't his to tell, like a betrayal. "I don't know why she picked him, but Frank was impossible to get rid of once he'd latched on to her. He wasn't going anywhere. Do you...do you think she needed to be with someone? Like it wasn't enough with just her and me? There, for a while, it even felt like she was picking him over me, because he was terrible to me. Terrible, Jake. He hated me something fierce. Mom, she... Do you think she'd have gone back to him? You think she'd have done that? Knowing what he was like? What he did to me? I can't tell you the number of times I couldn't go to school because of him."

"Because he beat you?" Jericho nodded instead of answering aloud. Jake's jaw tightened, a muscle in his cheek jumping as he asked, "That all he did to you?"

"He never...not like that. Not like you're thinking. But he was vicious. He killed a man in a bar fight a couple of years ago. Got drunk and beat a man to death. I read in the paper that the judge told him if he were a dog he'd be put down. I wish they would have put him down. I wish he'd died a long time ago. Does that make me a bad person?"

He remembered the news article he'd found in the library about the fight. The other man had started it, but once Frank started down a path, he didn't waver, not even when he'd beaten the man into a pulp. The reporter had noted the judge's hands were tied by a technicality but repeated the stern warning and harsh words directed to Frank verbatim.

"No, Jericho. That makes you human. Some people, people like Frank, they're bad in a way that can't be fixed. He broke your arm, the last in what sounds like a long list of brutality you had to endure at his hands over the years. Then even that wasn't enough. He came back and, honest to God, I really think he believed he'd killed you when he attacked you in the house. I think that's the only reason he didn't come back and finish the job. Those aren't the actions of a considerate person, not the actions of a good or just man. That's the way a monster behaves."

Jericho stared down at his lap, watching as dark splotches appeared, droplets of tears in a constant freefall from his face. Jake scooted closer and wrapped an arm around his shoulders, holding him steady.

"It was a monster that took your mother from you, Jericho. Not any action you did or didn't do. Not a thing except Frank was the cause. It's not your fault." He shook Jericho slightly and repeated himself, voice vibrating with intensity. "It's not your fault. It's not. The guilt lies directly at that man's feet, and if I had a say in it, he'd burn in hell forever. But it's not your fault."

They sat like that, the wet fabric of Jericho's jeans first becoming more saturated and then gradually drying in the sun and wind. Jake didn't hurry him, didn't say anything, just sat and held him against his side, the toes of one foot occasionally tapping out a rhythm to something only Jake could hear.

Jericho had focused on the rest area across the highway, servicing the traffic heading the other direction. He'd watched trucks weave into and out of it, their plumes of exhaust wafting away on the wind. Movement closer to hand caught his attention, and he saw Trent was stirring in the car.

"Uncle Trent's waking up." An earlier thought struck him, and he wondered silently for a moment, then decided to ask. "Should I...could I call you uncle, too?"

Jake's arm gave him a squeeze as the man took in a deep breath. He hummed, then nodded. "I'd be honored, Jericho. I would be honored." Jake released him and stood on the bench their feet had been propped on, stretching before waving at Trent, who was looking at them through the window, an owlish expression on his face.

Jericho smiled as he stood next to this man who had already shared so much wisdom with him, somehow knowing instinctively what Jericho needed to hear. He had a feeling the insights had been hard-earned, but even with the circumstances surrounding his meeting Trent and Jake, Jericho was glad.

"Okay. Uncle Jake it is."

Trent

"James, we're here." Trent turned to watch Jericho struggling with the strap on his duffel. It was on the tip of his tongue to ask Jacob to help him when he saw his husband walk around the back of the SUV and deftly snag the bag from Jericho, his smile at the boy defusing any argument. He didn't know what had happened at that rest area, but the changes seemed profound. Not that Jericho had been angry or obnoxious in any way before, but there had been a wall between where the boy stood and Trent and Jacob. Now, that wall was dust in the wind, and the backs of his eyes stung with remembered emotion from the moment he'd stepped out of the SUV and onto the rest area parking lot to be met by a lighthearted, "Sleep well, Uncle Trent?"

"Uncle Trent." He'd mouthed the words at Jacob over Jericho's head, getting a beaming grin in return.

It hadn't been a one-time thing either. After that moment, each time Jericho addressed him or Jacob, it was prefaced with the title Trent didn't know he'd longed for. Hadn't realized he'd been missing until it was gifted to him like that.

"James," he called again, shoving the door open wider to let Jacob pass through with their suitcase and Jericho's bag. Jericho followed, awkwardly angling his cast around where Trent stood.

Footsteps warned of an approach, and the lightness of the steps heralded the youngest of his nephews. Trent closed the door and watched as Jacob dropped the luggage he held and squatted with arms out. Matt didn't slow as he rounded the corner of the hallway, barreling full speed at Jacob, who scooped him up and stood, lifting him for a loud round of raspberries against his neck. The little boy burst into riotous giggles, noisily shouting at his uncle. Jaime was not far behind her son, and Jacob folded her into his arms, too, making Matt laugh more.

"Come here, James. Gimme, gimme, gimme some lovin'." Trent waded into the little knot of people he adored, peeling Jacob's arms away from Jaime with a roll of his eyes. "Hand her over already, honeybuns. Oh. My. God, you're so pretty when you're preggers. Well, you're beautiful all the time, but makin' babies sits well on you." He gave her a squeeze. "How are you doing, sweet girl?"

"I'm good." She hugged him tightly, then stepped back and dropped a hand to cover her belly. "We're good." Her gaze darted over his shoulder, and she pushed past him as Trent turned around, watching her move straight to where Jericho stood. Something about the boy's posture gave away his nervousness, and Trent got to watch that fade away as Jaime pulled him in for a hug, too. "Welcome, Jericho. We're so glad you're here." She looped her arm with Jericho's good one and turned them both to face Trent and Jacob. "We're grilling for supper. Con's already outside with Nate, so let's get your bags upstairs and head outside." She led Jericho towards the stairs, and Trent grabbed the duffel, leaving the suitcase for Jacob, who lifted it in one hand, the other still trapping Matt against his chest. Jaime was talking to Jericho, and Trent heard her say, "You're in the room with Nate. Jordan's supposed to be over tonight, but he usually crashes on the couch. You won't mind sharing, right?"

"No, ma'am." Jericho seemed to hesitate, and Trent knew why when he continued, "I don't mind, Aunt Jaime."

"Oh." Jaime's voice was soft, and she paused as they reached the stairs, one tread up from where Jericho stood, which put them at nearly the same height. "That's...that's good, Jericho. That's really good." Eyes sparkling suspiciously bright, she offered them all a trembling smile as she pulled Jericho on up the stairs. "That's really good."

A little while later, Trent and Jacob were in the guest room with the door closed. Jaime had shown Jericho to Nate's room first, then immediately led him away to go outside where Connor and Nate were. The smile she'd sent Trent's way said it was intentional, and he wasn't about to pass up the opportunity to have a few minutes alone with Jacob.

Chest plastered to Jacob's back, he leaned against him heavily, sighing out in a dramatic way he knew would have Jacob grinning. "Jakey, he called me uncle. That's amazing. I don't know what kind of voodoo you did do, but I like that you dooed it." He gave Jacob a tight squeeze, then sighed again. "Uncle Trentie and Uncle Jakey."

"He called James aunt, too. Did you see her face?" Jacob turned in his arms and locked Trent in an embrace before falling backwards, taking them both to the mattress.

Trent slipped to the side and curled up against Jacob, chin tilted up to look into his face. "She was stoked. I know Sammy calls her auntie, but to hear Jericho say it, that really meant something." He thought for a moment how to ask and had decided to just blurt it out when Jacob beat him to it.

"He's struggling with guilt, Trent. The boy's eat up with it, because he thinks it's his fault Frank killed Stella. Thinks it's his fault that she was with Frank to begin with. Hell, he thinks the fact she was killed in the barn was his fault, because he's the one who got them started boarding horses. He doesn't talk much, but when he does, even the little bit he shares is so telling. He's eaten up with guilt, and it doesn't stop with his mom." Jacob's hand drifted across Trent's cheek, fingers pushing his hair away from his face. "Nate texted me more, said Jericho hasn't given up on the idea that he owes us somehow for coming here for him. I can't disabuse him of that fact without throwing Nate under the bus, and I don't want to take away someone Jericho feels like he can talk to. Which means you and I have to get better at reading between the lines when he talks to us."

"That poor baby. I just want to wrap him up and keep everything in the world away. You think the guilt is because of how Stella raised him?" Trent couldn't imagine his sister doing anything intentionally, but he also was still struck by the idea that she'd kept Jericho a secret from him for nearly sixteen years. *Clearly Stella was capable of things I don't know.* "Or because of Frank?"

"Frank beat him." Jacob's expression was taut with an anger Trent didn't understand.

"Yeah, he broke his arm. Guy was an asshole."

"No. That wasn't the first of it, Trentie." Jacob's fingers moved through his hair again, in a steady soothing pattern at odds with the tension in his face. "Jericho said he had to miss school sometimes because of Frank."

Stunned, Trent lay still, his mind spinning as it tried to reconcile the sister he knew with one who might have ignored her own child's pain. "And you think Stella knew?"

"I do. I think she knew, and stayed. Maybe the arm was the worst of it, and that's why she'd said enough. We know she had a restraining order against him. Maybe it was the last straw, but from what Jericho told me today, there had been a lot of straws that came before. He asked me if I thought she would have picked him in the end." Jacob kept petting him soothingly, the sounds of his regular breaths helping Trent keep it together. "I didn't say anything against Stella. I know better." Jacob laughed softly, the lines in his face easing. "He defended you. We were talking about blame and I was trying to make a point and asked him if he hated you for not being there for him. That boy puffed up and shot me down in a heartbeat. He's a protector, and I love that about him. But I suspect it's why he got the brunt of Frank's abuse over the years. Probably some of what Frank would have directed Stella's way was taken on by Jericho. He's a good boy, Trentie. He's a good boy."

"What do we do?" Trent hated sounding so uncertain, but he knew if he put his fears out there, Jacob would build him up. Same as he would do for Jacob. "How can we help him?"

"I think we just love him. Give him time to come to terms with not just Stella's death, as devastating as that is, but also the knowledge that his mother, the person who should have been a hundred percent in his corner all the time, maybe wasn't." Jacob's lips thinned for a moment, and his gaze traced across Trent's face. "Just like you and I found that our parents didn't support us. Only ours was a huge blow all at once, like ripping off a bandage and letting the wound heal. Jericho's happened again and again. Tiny cuts, then big ones, but endless. Just over and over. I can't imagine it. I just can't. He's not going to be better in a day, or a week. Hell, maybe not even a year. But he'll be better, Trent. I promise you we won't stop loving him—and that love we'll show him, it'll move mountains."

"I do love him."

"I know you do. So do I. But he doesn't know it yet. Not in his bones. We've got to give it time to seep deep inside so he believes without a doubt that we have him." Jacob tilted his head and brushed Trent's lips with his. Trent hummed and smiled against his mouth, then chased him for a final light smacking kiss.

"We'll make it so he never doubts how we feel."

Trent just prayed his words came true.

Chapter Seven
Jericho

Waking slowly, Jericho blinked and stretched, staring at what was in front of him until it resolved into a wall about six inches away. He rolled to his back and was still so close to the wall his shoulder brushed it. The ceiling above him was some kind of complex texture. His befuddled brain turned random patterns into faces and outlines, becoming a game of sorts as he woke fully. He angled his head towards the other bed in the room, grinning at the blanket-covered lump that lay there. Not even Nate's hair was visible, the boy having burrowed so far under his covers he was completely hidden against the air-conditioned chill.

The dinner the night before had been a revelation unlike anything in Jericho's experience. He'd watched in awe as Jake's sister and her family acted out a fairy-tale evening of affectionate joking and teasing followed by games. Actual games that were played by everyone old enough to hold cards or move markers around a board—which meant only Matt was left out. And even then, Connor had pulled the boy into his lap and engaged him, having little Matt tell him which card to play next at one point.

The whole experience was so outside of anything Jericho had believed real families did that he nearly ruined it when Nate first brought out the board game, laughing hard. It wasn't until he'd seen the hurt on Nate's face that he'd realized the boy was serious, and then Jericho had wasted no time in admitting his mistake.

"Family game night's a thing? Really? Can we? Nate, you're not kidding, right?"

"You never played games with your mom?" Nate's words stung because they underscored the discrepancies Jericho had already noticed between what he and his mom had, and what Nate had with Jaime.

"Before supper was chores, after supper was cleanup." Jericho shrugged. "We didn't have the time."

Jaime closed in on Jericho's side, bumping him gently with her shoulder until he looked at her. "Well, now you do. Play a game with us, Jericho. It'll be fun. Promise."

"Okay, Aunt Jaime." He said it that way just to see the soft look on her face again when he gave her the title, and she didn't disappoint. Then she'd about knocked him on his butt when she'd leaned in and brushed his hair back from his face, placing a soft kiss against his temple that was as maternal as anything he'd ever experienced.

Over the course of the evening, Jericho had found that while the Thompson family as a whole were competitive, they had nothing on the Grimes siblings. Jake and Jaime had been cutthroat to each other, expending significant energy to block the other from advancing, even to the detriment of their own positions. About halfway through the first game, a smiling Trent had leaned close to whisper, "They're always like this. Get used to it."

The idea that he'd be around long enough to get used to it had filled Jericho with warmth, and he'd fumbled at the markers he had in his good hand. Nate had leaned close on his other side, offering to help, but Jericho had shaken his head, using the excuse of focusing on his next turn to cover the emotions that kept welling up inside him.

When it had grown late, Jericho had stumbled to bed alongside Nate, falling asleep without delay. His bladder complained now, making it known that he'd slept through the night, if the sun creeping around the curtains was to be believed.

He stretched again, then swung his legs off the bed, surprised when they landed on something soft. He leaned over and looked down to find his feet were in the middle of another blanket-covered lump on the floor. Drawing his feet back up, he stared down. Whoever it was, they were an adult—this wasn't a child sleeping on the floor between the two beds. *If not Matt, then who?* A glance at Nate reassured Jericho that he was still sleeping.

Quickly deciding which end was head and which feet, Jericho leaned over and plucked at the covers, wanting to pull them back just enough to know who it was. Only removing the blanket revealed a face he had never seen.

The young man was handsome, a wide, firm, scruff-covered jaw with just enough jut to telegraph masculinity. His light brown hair was tousled, streaks of sun-bleached blond threading through the thick mop. Thick lashes rested on his cheeks, and Jericho gave himself permission to trail his gaze down the man's neck, the notch between his collarbones giving off a feeling of exposed vulnerability. He had one hand shoved under a pillow, and even at rest, the corded tension in his forearm reflected what had to be a powerful physique.

Jericho swallowed hard, unsuccessfully willing his morning wood away.

Then the man sighed and moaned softly, shifting the slightest amount. His other hand appeared from under the covers, fingertips slipping up and across his chest, scratching lightly at the smattering of dark hair there. He moved again, and the bicep of the arm under the pillow bunched and flexed. The blanket pulled down to the man's waist, more than far enough for Jericho to see the tufts of hair under his arms, further proof of the masculinity and age of whoever this was.

Then the man opened his eyes, blinking sleepily, and Jericho flung himself backwards on the bed, trying to escape from view before the man found him staring like a weirdo. He misjudged the distance, though, head clonking against the wall with a thud. Lying still, he held his breath as he hoped it hadn't been enough for the man to have noticed.

No such luck. The top of the man's head appeared, but it was turned the other way, and Jericho heard a deep, sleep-roughened voice softly ask, "Nate? Was that you?"

Jericho looked across the room to see the blankets there had moved, too. Nate's face was framed in the opening, his gaze locked on Jericho. *Oh no*. Jericho glanced down his own body and saw the tent in his pajamas, flipping quickly to his side so he could hide it. *No, no, no.*

His movement made the man turn towards him, and it was only seconds before he was lost in a deep blue gaze. Something in his chest twanged, pulling taut in an almost painful way. The corners of those eyes crinkled, and Jericho didn't look away to verify, but he just knew the man was smiling. *At me.* "Hey." That same rough voice was directed at him this time, and Jericho found himself powerless to respond. "I'm Jordan." The blue vanished for an instant as the man, Jordan, blinked. Then those twin beams locked on Jericho again. "I'm Nate's bud. Jaime left me a note that they had guests. I'm guessing you're one of them?"

Nate must have seen Jericho's paralysis, because he offered, "He's Jericho, my new cousin. Uncle Trent and Uncle Jakey's nephew." The casual way Nate claimed him startled Jericho free from his trance, and he looked over, watching as the boy sat up, covers draped over his lap. "Why are you on the floor, Jordie?"

"Good to meet you, Jericho. Nate, the couch had two dogs on it. I couldn't bring myself to make the old guys leave their warm spots. Your dad keeps the house cold for early summer." Jordan sat up more, his bare shoulders coming into view, and they were exactly as broad as Jericho had thought they'd be. Bare and smooth, with toned muscles and so much skin on display Jericho didn't know where to let his gaze rest. He finally closed his eyes in self-defense only to have them pop back open immediately when the bed dipped next to him. Jordan had a hand on the edge of the mattress, using it as leverage to stand. He was directly in front of Jericho's face, and his boxer briefs didn't hide anything. The thick curve of his penis was right there, until it wasn't, but the view from the other side was just as gorgeous. He watched the muscles of Jordan's ass clench and shift as the man walked across to the door. "Gotta pee. Be right back." *I coulda done without the visual*. The idea that within only seconds Jordan would have his hands on—Jericho desperately tried to derail his thoughts.

"Jordan's in college." Jericho glanced at Nate, who was giving him a look he didn't know how to decode. "He's got a scholarship. Basketball. He used to play for Coach." Last night, Nate had alternated between calling Connor either Coach or Dad, and Jericho had learned his new uncle Con coached basketball at the local schools and had done so for more than a decade. Jericho figured it kinda made sense that one of Connor's favorite players would have been around enough to become friends with his son. "He's a good guy."

"You singin' my praises again, Nate?" Jordan pushed the door open with his shoulder, making his way into the room. He collapsed back onto the floor, tugging the blanket into his lap as if he were self-conscious. *I probably did that. He musta saw me staring at his junk*. Jordan leaned back on an arm and waved a hand grandly through the air, using a lofty tone as he said, "Don't let me stop you. Keep goin'. You're a gem, bud. A true treasure."

"Nah, just setting expectations." Nate's stare drilled into Jericho, and he nodded. *Message received. Eyes off the college friend out of my league*. "Jericho, how's the arm today?"

Jordan lifted his gaze from where he'd apparently been studying Jericho's shoes, placed on the floor at the foot of the bed. "What happened to your arm? Holy hell, that's an enormous cast. You break it?"

"Yeah." Jericho tried to look anywhere except at Jordan. The last thing he wanted to get into was how his arm came to be broken. "It's okay. Doesn't hurt much today."

"So I guess Trent and Jacob are your uncles? I've met them before. They're cool, especially Trent. He must be your mom's brother, right? Is your mom here, too? She enjoying her visit to Memphis? You guys see Graceland yet?"

The innocent questions rattled off in quick succession swept all the usable air out of the room, leaving Jericho gasping for breath. The need to retreat was overwhelming, and he fumbled with the covers as he stood. One-handed as he was, he had to keep attempting to untangle himself from them while already moving for the door, leaving the sheet and blanket strung out on the floor behind him. He didn't say anything, couldn't respond, wouldn't try to make himself even look at Jordan, unwilling to see the pity he knew would be on the gorgeous man's face in a minute, just as soon as he knew. The door to the bathroom clicked behind him, and Jericho leaned back against the welcome barrier, then slid down until his butt hit the floor, all the strength in his legs gone.

"Is your mom here, too?"

Chin to his chest, he fought the tears for a long time.

He lost.

Trent

Tapping on the door had Trent lifting his head off Jacob's shoulder and glaring through bleary eyes at the innocuous surface. "Go away."

Jacob snorted at his vicious whisper, then said in his normal morning voice, which was sexy-rough and entirely erection inducing, "Not sure they heard you, babe."

Elbow to the mattress, Trent pushed up on an arm and turned his glare on Jacob, who was grinning up at him. Without looking back at the door, he stated loudly, "Go away."

"Uncle Trent?"

That was Nate's voice. Trent's head dropped down, landing in the middle of Jacob's chest with a thud. He couldn't ignore their nephew, no matter how early it was. Trent lifted up and peered at Jacob's phone on the nightstand, then groaned softly. He turned his head so his cheek rested on Jacob's pec, and sighed heavily as Jacob's body jerked and shook underneath him. The man was not even trying to hide his laughter. "Yes, Nate?"

"Something happened."

Trent wasn't sure who moved faster, him or Jacob. He was scrambling over Jacob's body as his husband tried rolling out of bed, and only Jacob's grip on Trent's arms kept him from falling on his face. By virtue of an unintentionally well-placed shoulder, Trent knocked Jacob out of the way and reached the door first, yanking it open.

Nate's tiny, shocked "Eep" and the hand immediately covering the boy's eyes reminded Trent that while Jacob had put underwear on to sleep, he had not. He angled his body behind the door and tried not to shout at the boy. "What happened?"

Voice muffled, Nate told them, "Jericho's in the bathroom and he won't come out."

"Well…" Trent could think of three reasons for Jericho to have locked the younger boy out of the restroom but wasn't sure how to label them in an age-appropriate way. "Maybe he really has to go?"

Something brushed his foot as Jacob shouldered him aside and crouched in front of Nate.

"Nate, it's okay to look now. Uncle Trent's hiding behind the door." Trent saw Jacob had taken a moment to slip on a pair of sleep pants, and he looked down to see Jacob had brought him both underwear and Trent's favorite pair of sweats. "What happened, buddy?"

Trent ducked behind the door and started getting dressed, listening closely to their exchange.

"Jordie said something that upset him, and he ran out of the room."

Trent froze in place. Jordan was Nate's unconventional best friend, a boy he'd tutored through high school, even with Jordan being six years his senior. It was a testament to Jordan's good nature that he'd looked past Nate's age and into what made the boy tick, sticking around to help Nate through some of his hardest transitions.

"What did Jordan say to Jericho?" Jacob's tone was careful, level and calm, the entire opposite to how Trent felt this instant, and he knew it was a good thing Jacob had taken over the conversation with Nate. Trent's hands shook as he pulled the sweats up his legs, fighting against how they twisted around him. "You think it hurt his feelings?"

"We were just talking." The deeper voice had to belong to Jordan, and Trent rounded the edge of the door just as Jacob stood from the crouch he'd maintained. "I didn't know why he was with you guys. I thought maybe it was a family vacation or something. I asked about his mom."

Trent's forehead landed on Jacob's spine, now knowing what had happened. "I'll go." He pushed around Jacob, taking hold of his hand for a moment to squeeze, getting a tight grip in return. "You had no way of knowing, Jordie. It'll be okay." He clapped the young man on the shoulder, surprised when he was taller than Trent remembered. *He's growing up*. Nate turned anxious eyes towards him, and he ruffled the boy's hair. *Both of them are*. "It'll be okay," he said again.

The door to the bathroom closest to Nate's bedroom was closed, and Trent studied it for just a moment, listening intently. There was no sound of water running, no rustle of toweling off or getting dressed, and nothing else that would be considered bathroom activities. Fingers curled, he rapped gently against the wooden surface and, knowing that Nate and Jordan had probably been doing the same, he was not really surprised that he didn't get an immediate response.

He knocked again, just as softly, and asked, "Everything okay, Jericho?"

The door creaked, and from a position just below waist high, he heard Jericho say, "I'm fine, Tr—Uncle Trent."

The trembling hurt in Jericho's voice made Trent close his eyes, fighting the tears that had seemed far too close to the surface over the past days. Since he'd heard Reedman's voice on the phone telling him Stella had been murdered, his life had been a roller coaster, wildly swinging back and forth between terror and grief, and a deep and healing love for his newfound nephew. "I miss her, Jericho. I know that doesn't make sense, because I hadn't been able to spend any time with her for years, but just—" He turned and put his back to the door, sliding down until he was seated on the floor. "Just knowing I can't. Knowing that option has been taken away, no longer available, that's hard to wrap my head around sometimes."

"She would have loved these people. Seeing the friendship between Uncle Jake and Aunt Jaime would have made her smile." Jericho's voice broke even more, impossible shards of tragic pain shredding it until the sound warbled up and down the register, making him sound so much younger than he was. "It's not right that she's not here."

"You're right. It's not. That man took something precious from this world." Trent took a deep breath, then confessed. "I hate him. So much."

The doorknob rattled and clicked, and Trent shifted away as the door opened behind him. He turned to look into a still-crying Jericho's face. "I hate him too." Jericho sniffed loudly, then lost a bit of his tight control, a series of sobs breaking free. "I hate him. I wish I'd killed him. Killed him in his sleep. Come up behind him in the barn or something, stabbed him in the heart. I wish he was dead and she wasn't." The sobs turned into choking coughs, and Trent moved in to wrap the boy in his arms. Against his shoulder, Jericho said, "I could have saved her. I should have saved her. I didn't tell her everything. If she'd known him, what he could do, she would have left him sooner. I should have done something, Uncle Trent. I killed my mom."

"No, baby boy." He tightened his hold on Jericho, rocking them back and forth. "No, no, no. You didn't do this. Through action or inaction, none of it is your fault. Your mom wouldn't want you to think that, and she'd be right. It's not your fault. You can't blame yourself. You can't. If you're going to blame someone, blame me." Jericho jerked, but Trent didn't relax his grip, keeping him close to his chest. "I should have known something wasn't right when I met him at our parents' funeral. I shouldn't have left her alone. I should have been there for her."

"It's not your fault, Uncle Trent." Jericho's wail filled the hallway, and Trent pressed a kiss to the boy's head.

"Love you for that, sweet boy. I know it's not my fault, but neither is it yours. You're going to have to let that go. Hold on to the grief, hold on to the love you have for her, but let that part of the pain go." Footsteps shuffled in the hallway behind them, and Trent looked back to see Jacob, Jordan, and Nate all standing in the doorway to the bedroom, only steps away. "You've got a whole bunch of people who want nothing more than to help you get through this, Jericho. Let that self-blame pain go and use us to work through what's left. It's a huge loss, baby boy. Sweet baby boy, you lost your mother. That hurts so badly I bet it's like you can't breathe sometimes. Don't torture yourself with even more."

Jacob stepped over them and into the bathroom. Trent watched as he located and wet a washcloth, gathered up a handful of tissues, and then came to sit on the floor at Jericho's back, sandwiching the boy between them. *And that's one of the reasons I love that man more than life.* Jacob always knew the right things to do or say, and seeing him take on a protector role over Jericho was like getting a tiny glimpse into the kind of father he would make one day.

After a long time, Jericho's sobs started to trail off and he stirred restlessly. Trent leaned into Jacob's hand when he cupped his cheek, then saw Jericho do the same as Jacob transferred that quiet affection to their nephew. They shuffled Jericho between them, and Jacob tenderly washed Jericho's face, placing the tissues into the boy's hand. Jacob tossed the wet cloth into the sink, then motioned to where Nate and Jordan still stood. A moment later, the boys were on their knees next to the trio, and without saying a word, added their arms to the ones circling Jericho.

"Lean on us," Trent whispered into Jericho's ear. "We'll help you keep it together, and when you can't, like right now, if you let us, we'll help you fall apart."

Jericho

"Hey."

The soft greeting came from behind Jericho, and he squeezed his eyes shut, irrationally hoping that if he ignored Jordan, the man would disappear. Poof, gone, along with all the embarrassing memories of the previous day.

He'd been so exhausted from his freak-out that he'd willingly stayed in Nate's bedroom most of the day, only coming out at dinner. The conversation around the table hadn't required anything from him, and Jericho had finished his meal quickly, slipping away early. He'd pretended to already be asleep when Nate came in later, and the instant he'd heard Nate talking to Jordan, Jericho had been glad he'd stooped to the pretense to keep from having to talk to anyone.

"Jericho."

The sound of his name in that smooth voice made Jericho's heart lurch in his chest. He bit down on the inside of his bottom lip, turned his face to the side away from Jordan, and stayed as still as he could. *Maybe I'll disappear.*

"I hope you can forgive me for yesterday."

Jericho jerked his head up and twisted to look at the man. Jordan stood close to him, well within arm's length. All Jericho would have to do was take a single step to the side and he'd be pressed up against him. Jordan wasn't looking at him, chin down, his gaze fixed on the span of floor between where they stood.

"I didn't know. I never would have hurt you. I'm sorry."

Jericho opened his mouth, but nothing came out, his voice locked away, imprisoned by the memory of not just the pain but the humiliation of Nate and Jordan seeing him like that. Sitting on the floor of a bathroom, tears and snot and whatever else was part of bawling his eyes out. Like a child, a baby, not at all like someone who'd been standing tall in the face of everything Frank had thrown at him through the years. His brain shouted at him that Jordan's apology was just a way for him to shield Jericho from knowing how embarrassed he was on Jericho's behalf at being found out like that.

"Anyway, I gotta head out. I've got early classes tomorrow, and I still have studying to do." Jordan made an aborted gesture, his hand rising and reaching out to Jericho but stopping short of contact, falling away as he turned and walked towards the doorway. "Was good to meet you, Jericho."

"You, too." His mouth finally caught up with his mind, and he forced the words out, surprised when Jordan paused in the door to look back. Their gazes clashed, and just as it had the morning before, Jericho's chest contracted, that connecting thread pulling tight around his suddenly speeding heart. "Drive safe, Jordan."

The impossibly blue eyes crinkled at the corners as Jordan smiled at him. "Jordie. My friends call me Jordie." With a graceful chin lift and a flip of his fingers, Jordan was gone.

Jordie. He'd used the name mentally before, but having been granted permission like this meant it felt like the first time.

Chapter Eight

Trent

"Uncle Jake, next time can I just give him a poke?"

Trent kept his eyes closed as he smiled, face angled away from where the voice came from. He was coiled in the back seat of the SUV, propped up by a pillow shoved in the corner by the door. His latest nap had ended just moments before when a jarring bump had rattled him free from sleep. He'd never accuse Jacob of waking him on purpose, but Jericho's comment certainly put the move under suspicion.

"I'm awake." He lifted his chin as he yawned, turning his head in time to catch Jacob's gaze in the rearview mirror. "Hey, you scrumptious thing you." Straightening up, he looked outside, seeing the road framed the familiar view of the ocean to the west, and mountains far in the distance on the east. "Oh, you made good time, honeybuns."

"Promised you that we'd sleep in our bed tonight." Jacob's voice was gruff and strained, and when Trent looked closer, it was clear how tired he was. "I keep my promises."

Leaning forwards, Trent trailed his fingers across the back of Jacob's neck, finding the strain of tense muscles and rubbing small circles over those sensitive spots. "I know you do, Jakey. Not long now and we'll all be home." He caught Jericho looking at them with a sappy grin on his face and smiled back at the boy.

Jericho had done well on their extended road trip, proving a good traveler who was considerate of others in the vehicle. Trent and Jacob had shared a hushed and hurried conversation during their shower last night, comparing notes on Jericho's continued odd behavior after they'd left Memphis. He'd been good, sure. But Trent was convinced it was too good, with no emotional outbursts or even grumpy moments. Jacob had felt the boy just needed to settle into a routine, understandably thrown off by everything that had happened.

Trent thought it was more, but he'd backed off his desire to have a conversation with Jericho then and there, grudgingly admitting to Jacob that he might be right about a small hotel room in a nowhere town in the middle of Nevada being the wrong place to tackle what could prove to be a sensitive subject.

"Any state parks between us and home?" Trent angled his head at the glove box, where the stash of paper maps they'd bought Jericho had taken up residence. When Jacob found out Jericho had never been to a park of any kind, their route from Memphis to San Diego had grown exponentially longer. "Didja check a map?"

First it was the mountains and forests of Arkansas, then the reservations of northern Oklahoma. They'd dipped into Texas at some point to see a line of cars half-buried in the red dirt, and then headed back along I40 to weave their western way to the Grand Canyon. Jacob and Jericho had pored over the maps every night, planning the next day's travel. It had been amazing to see them bonding over something as simple as ink and paper, the shine in their eyes worth any amount of uncomfortable quarters in motels and the car.

Jericho had taken things a step farther, beginning at the first park. He'd asked a ranger to sign his cast, prompting Trent to realize neither he nor Jacob had signed it yet. The Thompsons and Jordan had, but those were the only, lonely signatures on the entire expanse. Trent had been angry at himself over that, because it was such a stereotypical thing to do: sign a kid's cast to memorialize a broken bone. Now the cast was covered end-to-end with signatures in all colors and quality of penmanship, a piece of history to mark their first-ever family trip. Not a vacation, not with the reason they were together in the first place, but it would be something Jericho could keep if he wanted.

Jericho rolled his eyes and Trent had a hard time controlling his laughter when he saw the expression on the boy's face. The communicative eye roll was something Jericho seemed to have picked up from him, and it drove Jacob crazy. He claimed it made them look like they were twins when they did it at the same time. Something Jericho found hilarious, given the beard Trent sported and his own smooth jaw.

"I think Uncle Jake just wants to get home." Jericho grinned at Trent.

"You'd be correct, young man."

Jacob maneuvered the vehicle to the outside lane on the freeway, and Trent saw they were nearing their exit. A few moments later, they were off the highway and onto the surface streets, blocks blurring by as he took in the familiar sights. He yawned and was scrubbing at his face with his palms when Jericho made a pained sound. They were stopped at a red light, and Jericho was staring out the passenger window, fingers clutching at his knee until his knuckles were white and strained. Looking past the boy, Trent saw they were just up the street from one of the more popular gay clubs, the line to get in stretching down the block and around the corner. Whatever was distressing Jericho was in that line, men in various versions of club attire everywhere. The club catered to a wide variety of tastes, which meant there were twinks in sparkly short-shorts standing next to leather cubs in harnesses, and lumbersexual bearded men alongside bow-tied geeks.

Trent turned to see Jacob watching Jericho, too. He shrugged and looked back at traffic, easing the car through the light when it turned green. From the corner of Trent's eye, he saw Jericho move and angled his head to watch as the boy strained to keep his gaze on the line, twisting in his seat to stare back at the intersection and the throngs of men until it was entirely lost to view.

Trent sat back in the seat before Jericho could notice he'd been watching, relaxing in the knowledge that within a few minutes they'd be home.

Jericho

Angling his good arm across his body, Jericho fumbled with the door handle for a moment before it opened and he could swing his legs out of the car to stand. The cast was in the way as always, and he held it awkwardly away from his body as he turned to lean back into the car, picking up and stuffing things from the console and floor into a bag Jake had tossed his way at their last snack stop. He smiled. Both Trent and Jake had seemed focused on getting him to eat, approaching the idea of fattening him up as if it were a critical mission, even if their trajectories were very different. Jericho had found that not having access to much junk food up to now had cultivated a palate that preferred healthier and more natural things instead of gas station donuts and bags of bulk candy—much to Jake's pleasure and Trent's dismay.

Standing beside the car, he closed the door and looked around at the house and surrounding property. Not large, the one-story home sat far back from the street, the front yard stretching out to the sides as a buffer between it and the neighboring homes. He mentally compared the tidy house with its soft cream and crisp blue paint, with the rental he'd lived in with his mom, wondering what Trent and Jake had thought when they had first seen it. Cracked paint, angled boards holding up the porch, windows painted shut. Even the inside of that house had been tired and old, rundown and worn.

"Come on," Jake called from where he stood on the porch that stretched the width of the building. The door was open, and Trent had disappeared, already inside the cool depths of the house and away from the heat. Jericho glanced down at himself, seeing the new jeans and shirt that his uncles had bought him, but on his feet were the same ratty, cheap sneakers he'd worn for more than a year. His toes were scrunched into the end, feet grown so wide the laces were scarcely long enough to tie anymore. He flashed to Jordan seated on the floor of Nate's room. Jordan had been staring at his shoes, and he understood why now. They didn't go with houses like this one, or Jaime and Connor's house in Memphis. These shoes, which he'd kept because they felt more like himself than any of the ones his uncles had purchased, didn't fit in with this weird and unwelcome life he found himself thrust into.

An unexpected wave of anger washed over him. Not at Trent or Jake, not Jaime or Connor—at his mom. If she hadn't picked a loser like Frank, their life might have been different. He'd used her instead of contributing, and she hadn't cared that it literally took food off the table for Frank to keep up with his latest obsession—be that case after case of beer, an expensive bottle of booze, or those stinky stogies he smoked. *We'd have been a lot better off without him.* It was as if his mother had picked herself over Jericho, which wasn't how he wanted to remember his mom. That anger twisted and turned, folding back on itself inside him until he was furious with himself. *I coulda done better*. He hadn't, and he remembered throwing words at her in their last big fight. He'd never tossed out an "I hate you," but his tone had carried the same amount of rage and vitriol; it felt like he might as well have.

"Jericho? You coming, son?"

His head jerked up, and he stared at Jake, who was still standing in the doorway, patiently waiting. He gave the impression he'd wait forever if that's what Jericho needed. It had been the same since he'd met the two men. Both Trent and Jake had given him time whenever he needed it. They'd stood with him, sometimes holding him and sometimes seeming to read that he'd shatter if touched with compassion. But they'd been there, and with every moment and movement, his unexpected uncles had reinforced their words, the plainly spoken statements they'd made to him that he had a place with them, they were happy to have him, and they'd always give him a place to land. *Son*. Hearing the affectionate word from Jake, who spoke as eloquently with logical arguments as he did emotional discussions, simply underscored how effortlessly they fitted him into their lives.

"Yeah." His voice creaked and groaned around the short word, as if he hadn't spoken in years, as if it were a gate hinge in dire need of oiling. "I'm coming, Uncle Jake." Each word came easier, and that earned him a quick smile, a thing he'd come to look for. When Jake was truly pleased and smiled, he did it with his whole face, even his body language changing and softening. Uncle Trent was the same way, his every emotion written on his face, and in him, Jericho had finally understood the expression "wears his heart on his sleeve." That fit Uncle Trent to a T. "Nice place." Jericho gave an understated assessment but knew Jake read between the lines and got everything he couldn't find words to say.

"Yeah, it's nice." Jake glanced around, pride in his every move. "We like it."

"You have a lawnmower?" Jericho lifted the cast and shrugged. "When this comes off, I can take over mowing. I can do whatever you need." He hated the desperation in his voice, but that wagonload of emotional bricks had again hammered home to him how much Trent and Jake were changing their lives to make room for him. "You name it."

"We'll see in three weeks when that comes off." Jake jerked the top of his head towards the opening, stepping back to hold the door wide. "Come on. I wanna get my shoes off and sit on my ass for a minute in a chair that's not vibrating my balls off. Trent's getting your room ready now."

Yeah, Uncle Trent's having to scramble to make a place for me, because when they left to come to Tennessee, they hadn't intended to bring me back.

Something of his thoughts must have shown on his face as he trudged towards the house, because Jake turned loose of the screened door, letting the pneumatic arm close it softly behind him as he stepped towards the edge of the porch, meeting Jericho there. "Don't, Jericho. Don't do that to yourself. I don't know what's going on in your head, but just don't. We want you here." *Well, that proved he's a mind reader.* "If we didn't, we wouldn't have raised both hands and yelled 'Pick me, pick me' when the judge was making his ruling. We *want* you with us. It's where you belong, and neither Trent nor I would have it any other way. You're stuck with us now, kiddo. No way around it." Jake angled down so he was staring right in Jericho's face, the passion imbued in his gaze slightly unnerving, but Jericho steeled himself to meet it, in the end seeing only concern and sincerity there. "You're ours. It doesn't matter if you mow the yard or not." Jake gave a one-shouldered shrug and grinned, breaking the intense mood slightly. "I won't argue with you if you *want* to mow it, but don't feel like that kind of thing is how you have to pay your way. We, me and Trent, we aren't going to get tired of you or decide you're too much trouble. We aren't going to leave you, and we will not, will *never* let you leave. This is us, and now *us* includes *you*."

Trent had been hovering in the doorway, his expression obscured by the screen until he shoved it wide and Jericho saw he was blinking away tears. "Get used to it, Jericho. Jacob's never wrong when it comes to family. Never trust his selections at a sushi bar, but where family is concerned, he's the master of making things make sense."

"Okay." Jericho shrugged and glanced down, embarrassed he'd forced them to have yet another emotional conversation with him, just to soothe his nerves. A huge part of him wanted to apologize, but he knew Jake would meet any "I'm sorry" with a demand to know what he'd done wrong, and then it would become even more of a thing than it was. He decided the best way to let them both know he'd heard and was digesting their messages was to move things along and follow Jake's earlier directive. "Uncle Trent, can you show me my room? Uncle Jake said his balls were still vibrating, and he needed you to look at them." Jake snorted a laugh, and Jericho looked up to see Trent's mouth opened in a distorted "O". "I'm pretty sure that's going to involve things I don't want to see, so I thought I could put my stuff away while you guys did…whatever."

"Jesus, kid." Jake reached out and grabbed the edge of the door from Trent. "Get your ass inside already." His gruff words were at odds with the smile on his face, and Jericho deliberately bumped his shoulder into this found uncle, someone he hadn't known he needed in his life.

As he stepped inside, he took a moment to marvel at the changes from even a month past. Of course his mother was gone, and that would be a pain he carried with him all his days, because, soul deep, he missed her. But beyond that, he'd gone from a boy who had a narrow thread of family to someone with uncles and an aunt and cousins, open invitations to come stay in Memphis if Jake and Trent decided not to move back, and an offer to tour Jordan's college and meet his friends.

"Blessed beyond measure."

He wasn't aware he'd muttered the words, a saying from Bible study that his grandmother had taught him, until

Trent's hand lifted and cupped the back of his neck, bringing their faces close together. Staring into Jericho's eyes, Trent finished the phrase, bringing things full circle in Jericho's mind. "Forever and ever, amen."

Hours later, he was sprawled out on one of the two couches in the living room, Trent and Jake seated on the other in something he couldn't call anything except what it was: a cuddle. They'd just finished watching a fourth episode of some show he couldn't get into, but he also couldn't complain about the way the characters dressed, because every man in the show was fine.

Without thinking, something that had been happening more and more often over the past weeks since leaving Knoxville, he asked, "Those men in the street today, was that like a parade or something?"

When they'd first stopped at the red light, he'd been facing the other direction, but Jake had glanced past Jericho's shoulder and grinned, then lightly shook his head as he faced front again. Intrigued at what could pull that kind of reaction from his uncle, Jericho had turned to look and been floored. If he'd been standing, he would have been taken to his knees.

Men, with only a couple of exceptions, and it had only taken a little studying to realize even they weren't really exceptions, just dressed differently. Men in sparkly rainbow tank tops, hair curling and shining in the sun. Men with no shirts, their chests strapped with leather belts and buckles, tight pants of the same material wrapped around their butts and legs. Men who dressed like Marco, a little upscale but comfortable, light pastel colors complementing their golden tans. Men, so many men, all pressed together so when one took a step backwards the others around had to adjust to allow it, bodies brushing against each other. He was reminded all at once of the magazine he'd stolen from the gas station only a month ago, the ad for the club inside the front cover promising man meat everywhere.

That led immediately to a memory he'd tried to repress, that of Frank's eyes drilling into him over the glowing ember of the cigar, smoke wreathing the man's head as if looking for the horns of a devil. Heart racing, he struggled, trying to force the fear away, hoping his uncles wouldn't see.

That prayer was answered, at least, because when Trent responded to the question Jericho had already forgotten asking, he only sounded amused, not alarmed.

"No, baby boy. Not a parade. Just a line to get into one of the clubs."

Jericho looked at Trent, seeing he was still staring at the TV. Jake, watching Jericho, wore an expression of concern. Jericho tried smiling at him, hoping to forestall whatever observation Jake had been about to make. It worked, thankfully, because Jake gave him a short nod, then tightened his arms visibly around Trent. The squeeze got Uncle Trent's attention, but by the time he looked at Jericho, Jericho was sure he'd been able to blank his face convincingly.

"A club? Like a dance club?"

Trent grinned and nodded, then leaned his head back against Jake's shoulder. The two men had been significantly freer with their affection since getting back into their own home, and that made him wonder how hard it had been to curtail it back in Tennessee.

"So, like, that's a thing? A dance club for guys?" Jericho let loose a little snort of amusement. "That's pretty cool. They're pretty brave to just, I don't know, stand there where anyone could see and know that they were going to the club like that."

"California's more progressive than Tennessee, that's for sure." Trent was watching the TV again, but Jericho saw his mouth twist sideways. "'Free to be me' was a motto for a political candidate not long ago, and I always thought that summed up Southern California in a nutshell. Sure, SanFran has a higher ratio of gays to straights, but it's less politicized here. It just is, instead of something to aim for."

"Did you ever live in San Francisco?"

Jake shook his head. "We went from Memphis to San Diego, living down near Coronado to start with. Such a tiny, jankie little apartment, and we still paid through the nose. But the views?" That broad grin came back and Jericho responded in kind, feeling the corners of his mouth curl up. "I'd never seen the ocean, never played in the sand before we came out here. I was ready to pay twice as much just for the chance of seeing the ocean every morning."

"And the other scenery wasn't bad, either." Trent chuckled. "It's a Navy town, so there were—" Trent made a choking sound that morphed into a series of muffled snorts when he laughed harder, hardly able to get the words out as he finished with, "There were seamen everywhere."

"Ah, God. That's so bad. It wasn't funny the first time you said it, Trentie." Jake had thrown his head back, laughing raucously at the ceiling. He raised his voice an octave and lilted a nonsense response, "Seamen, seamen, seamen. There was seamen everywhere."

Jericho watched them laugh, each man offering varying versions of the same phrase, their laughter growing more hysterical and out of control, and he was just sitting like a lump because none of it made sense to him. Embarrassed, he finally admitted on a soft mutter, "I don't get it."

"Ah, God." Jake flung a hand up, waving it side to side in a negating motion. "Flag on the field, Trentie. You gotta take this one. I can't."

"No, Jakey. Please. Don't make me. I'll puke if I laugh more." Trent had slumped down, his head in Jake's lap, fingers wiping tears from under his eyes. "Please."

"No, this is all you, babe."

"Oh, man." Trent made a visible effort to get himself under control, losing it and convulsing with laughter again. The whole time Jericho felt himself getting stiffer, muscles tensing up, because as with everything in Tennessee, he was on the outside, not in the know, different. "Okay. Navy guys are called seamen, right?" Trent lifted his head and looked at Jericho, who nodded. "And jizz," Trent gave a rolling wave aimed vaguely over his middle, "is also called semen." The play on words hit Jericho then, and he stared at Trent with wide eyes, not moving, not blinking. Trent muttered, "Oh, Jakey. I broke him."

Jericho flung himself to the side as heat flooded his face, and he pressed tight to the cushions at the back of the couch as peal after peal of laughter burst out of him. "Semen everywhere."

"Exactly." Trent's shout was threaded through with hilarity, and the room echoed with Jake's laughter, too. "So much semen. So funny. All the semen."

After the laughter finally died down, and Trent stopped muttering "semen" at odd intervals, Jericho pushed up to a sitting position, staring over at Trent and Jake. "Did you guys ever go to a club like that? A dancing club for me?" Eyes wide, he corrected himself quickly. "*Men*, I mean. A dancing club for men?"

"Yeah, we did." Jake dropped his head to smile at Trent. "My husband can cut a rug. We spent many an evening in places just like that one."

"Did it... Were you scared the first time you went inside one?"

Trent pursed his lips, thinking, then said, "Not really. Not once we got into the line, because the energy was just so positive. As if everyone there understood exactly what was in my head. It felt like I'd found my tribe." He wrinkled his nose and narrowed his eyes to look up at Jake, who was watching the TV. "At least until I found a twinky boy pressed all up against my man. I told him to take his go-go-boots-wearing self somewhere else."

"He wasn't my type, babe." Jake didn't look down, but he reached for Trent's hand, their fingers falling into place. "I like 'em beefy."

"I got your—" Trent shot a glance at Jericho as he interrupted himself. "Jakey, watch the show."

"I am." The soft smile Jake aimed at the TV wasn't lost on Jericho.

I wish Mom could have seen this. Just this. It could have changed everything.

Chapter Nine
Trent

"Thank you. Yes, I'll hold." Tapping the tip of a pencil against the tablet laid on the counter in front of him, Trent studied the remaining list he'd written out last night, sighing at how few had been checked off. The legal aspect of taking on a not-quite-sixteen-year-old boy was proving daunting, but fortunately, Mr. Reedman had provided him information about not only what kind of documentation he'd have to provide the courts, but also hooked Trent up with the names of a couple of family lawyers back in Knoxville. He and Jacob had hired one here in California, too, and while both lawyers had reassured Trent this was a very straightforward case, it still needed the official stamp of approval.

He'd expected home visits, interviews, and the like, but it was the more intangible things that kept tripping him up.

Like what he was trying to do right now, setting Jericho up with a doctor. The cast was only a week away from needing to be removed, and he was on with the fourth doctor's office, hoping to find one that would accept a new patient on such short notice.

There was a sound on the line, and he perked up, mouth open to respond, when the noises flattened and went away. He pulled the phone from his head and looked at it, frowning. The screen was dark and pushing buttons didn't do anything. "Dammit." Either the phone had died entirely, or it had run out of battery, but either way, it meant he wasn't any closer to finding an answer to the pressing problem.

"*Jakey.*" He directed his yell towards the back of the house, where their joint office was. No answer, which meant Jacob probably had his headphones on, intently working. Interrupting him would mean derailing Jacob's productivity for a while, because it took time to get back into the groove. Trent twisted to look towards the front of the house, where he knew Jericho was in the living room watching something on TV. A buzz on the table behind him drew his attention, and he saw the phone they'd bought for Jericho lying there, the screen's brilliance fading from a recent notification.

Problem solved, he thought, proud of himself for dealing with it and not having to bother Jacob.

He fumbled with the device, expecting to have to unlock it somehow, but the screen brightened again as soon as he pushed the first button. In the middle of what he saw was a text message. It was a thread Jericho had with Nate, and while not every message talked about not wanting to be a burden, it was certainly a theme throughout each of them he skimmed. He navigated away from that conversation and saw Jordan's name was actually first on the list of most recent threads. There were a number of notifications, indicating unread messages. While he was trying to decide how he felt about the older boy, a young man really, texting his nephew, another message came in and flashed up on the screen.

I rlly wish yd answr me. I dbl cked w Nate so I kno I got the # rght. Talk 2 me Jericho.

Blowing out a stream of air, he angled his head up and minimized the text application. He still wasn't sure what it meant that Jordan was reaching out, but Jericho was ghosting him. That didn't seem like the boy he was coming to know and love. But admitting he'd seen anything would be an invasion of privacy, which would undoubtedly cost him no small amount of the trust he'd built up with the boy in just a few short weeks.

Glancing down at the phone number written on the paper in front of him, he tapped it into the phone and connected, laying the device down and putting it on speaker. Ringing ended and the call immediately went to an auto-attendant, and he worked his way through the various menus until he was back in the queue for scheduling. Tonight would be soon enough to ask Jacob how best to handle the things Trent had read, and then strategize about how to deal with the other.

Appointment successfully made, Trent had moved to the next series of calls, establishing guardianship through the school system, because it was likely Jericho would have to at least start the school year here in San Diego. As he was rattling off his email address for what felt like the hundredth time today, lips landed on the back of his neck, and a well-known hand slipped across his chest, Jacob's strong arm pulling Trent backwards until he rested against his husband.

"Uh-huh." He wiggled against Jacob, getting more comfortable while prompting the woman on the phone to keep talking, hoping she'd get to the point sometime soon. "Yes, ma'am, but when do we need to have his transcript from Tennessee?" More rambling words, until finally she stumbled into disclosing the information he needed.

"No later than one week before registration. The guidance counselors will want time to provide the best possible advice for his academic success."

"Okay, I think we can do that." He jotted the dates down, drawing a heavy, black circle around the deadline. "Thank you so much."

Trent ended the call and locked the phone, tossing it facedown on the countertop next to his own. Jericho had received another half a dozen texts while Trent used the phone, and he'd studiously tried to ignore each one.

"You done working, honeybuns?" Trent lifted his chin as he spoke, looking into Jacob's face from his position on the stool. Jacob swooped down and brushed his lips lightly across Trent's, pulling a smile and a contented hum from him. *My hunka-hunka.*

"Yeah. The team's done amazing. I can't believe we're already caught up on everything I missed during our trip." Jacob kissed him again, and Trent closed his eyes, falling into the caress until Jacob pulled back and ended it with a series of tender, closemouthed pecks. "What do you want for supper, babe? I'm cooking tonight."

"Ugh, work. I can't even think about that right now. I can't. Not now. I made all the calls we needed, I think. It's so much, Jakey. But Jericho's lined up for a doctor early next week to remove the cast. The appointment is with a guy who's in a decent pediatrician group. I finally found a bunch of good recommendations online. Then when I talked to Carla from the ad agency, I found out it's where she takes her teenaged son, so they're used to more than just babies."

"That last call was the school?" Jacob's arms loosened as Trent sagged forwards, elbows to the countertop.

He nodded, then rolled his neck side to side. "Yeah. They need a whole *list* of things. It just doesn't end. Mr. Reedman promised to help expedite some of it, by virtue of his cousin being the superintendent where Jericho went to school last year. I'll never get over how efficient the backdoor connections still are in a place like Knoxville." He shook his head, tiredly threading his fingers through his hair. "The idea of doing this all over again in just six months is killer, Jakey. I never knew there was so much to it all."

"You'll manage." Jacob kissed up the back of Trent's neck until his nose was buried in Trent's hair. "You're good at this kind of thing." The vibrations from his words tickled, and Trent lurched away. "Babe."

"Memphis? Do we really want to think about moving back there, Jakey? I didn't realize how careful we were in Knoxville and there until we were back home. I want to be able to touch you, to kiss you. To damn well hold your *hand* if I want to." Trent knew he was being dramatic, but it was what they did. He stretched things until they didn't resemble reality, taking it over the top until Jacob brought everything back into perspective. "We like the surrogacy clinic here, our friends are here, and now Jericho's doctor and school are here. Should we uproot him, and ourselves, just to move across the country to a place where I can't even hold my husband's hand?"

"Trent, babe." Jacob's hand curled across Trent's chest again, fingertips grazing across a nipple as warm lips and hard teeth ran down his neck.

"This isn't a 'babe' situation, Jakey." Trent arched his throat, silently asking for more, sighing as Jacob's teeth sank into the tender tissue at the crook of Trent's neck.

"*Au contraire*, I think every situation is a 'babe' situation, if I get the tone just right." The fingertips circled his nipple, then came together in a light pinch. "Babe."

"Mmhmm. Yeah, maybe that's the right 'babe,' right there." Trent shifted on the stool, his half-hard cock uncomfortable in his jeans. "Except I thought you were going to cook?"

"I am." Jacob pressed against Trent's back, mouth working along his neck again. "I think the kitchen's already getting hotter."

"Uh, honey?" Trent reached back, gripping Jacob's hip to pull him even closer. "The kitchen's over there."

"Yeah?"

"What's for supper?" Jericho's voice wasn't close, but the reminder they weren't alone in the house was like a splash of cold water across Trent's nerves.

"To be continued," Jacob murmured, as he pressed a final kiss to the side of Trent's face.

"Oh my Jesus." Trent muttered as he shifted again, shivering in the sudden chill as Jacob moved away, taking his heat with him. "Uncle Jacob's cooking, so you know what that means."

"Pizza or pasta." Jericho was laughing softly, smiling as he walked into the room. He glanced at the kitchen table, and his eyes went wide. Then he turned back to the living room.

"I've got your phone. I had to use it. Mine died." Trent picked up what he thought was his, but the screen was lit up with another handful of texts from Jordan. "Here's yours, Jericho. Looks like Jordan's chatty tonight. I'm glad you've got a friend like him."

"Oh, we're not—" Jericho took the phone from Trent's fingers and didn't look at it, just shoved it deep into his front pocket. "It's not anything, really. Hey, want me to get you a charger cord, Uncle Trent?"

"Nice deflection, kiddo." Jacob chuckled as he walked around the counter and into the kitchen.

Trent watched Jericho's face turn white before a rosy hue flooded up his cheeks. "Totally deflecting." That got Jericho's gaze back on him, and he softened their teasing with a smile. "Jordie's a really good kid."

"He's not a kid." Jacob offered this nugget from where he stood in front of the refrigerator, door open as he looked through the selection. "We need to go shopping." He closed the refrigerator, then opened the pantry door, head shifting up and down as he scanned the shelves. "There's nothing to make for supper."

"Of course he's a kid. I remember when he and Nate graduated from high school." Trent pushed off the stool and walked around to where Jacob was, bumping their shoulders together. "You wanna call for pizza or me?"

"Jordan's in his second year of college. He's not a kid. He's a man. Doesn't matter if he and Nate graduated on the same day, there's a solid six years' difference between their ages." Jacob backed away and leaned a hip against the counter near the sink, phone in hand. "I've got it. I told you I'd take care of supper."

"No, you said you'd cook." Trent pressed a kiss against Jacob's shoulder, looking up and batting his eyes in a way he knew Jacob found adorable. "Calling for pizza isn't cooking."

"Yeah, this is Jacob Grimes, and I need to place an order for delivery." Away from the phone, Jacob huffed a laugh, then told Trent, "It counts, babe."

Trent closed the pantry and turned to see Jericho had brought the phone back out and was staring down at it with a look of growing fear.

"Everything okay, Jericho?"

The boy's head jerked up, and he stared at Trent. In the background, Jacob gave the pizza place his credit card information. The expression on Jericho's face faded away, growing blank as he nodded. In a voice way too chirpy for what Trent had just seen, Jericho tried to assure him, "Yeah, Uncle Trent. Right as rain."

Not believing that for a second.

Casually, he tried to reintroduce the topic Jericho was dodging earlier. "How are Jordan's classes this semester? He's taking two over the summer, right?" Trent studied Jericho's face carefully. "He'll be back home soon for a break before fall. Maybe we should go back for a visit while he's home."

If possible, Jericho's face turned whiter than before. His headshake was jerky, an uneven side-to-side movement.

Trent decided to take pity on the boy, because if what he was seeing was true, Jericho was harboring a healthy crush on the handsome young man. Another thing to talk over with Jacob once they went to bed.

"Pizza will be here in twenty minutes." Announcement made, Jacob curled his fingers around Trent's wrist, and he went with the tug, leaning against Jacob's side without argument. "I'm going to take a shower and change." Pressure against the side of Trent's head was a kiss, and he sighed when Jacob bent close, mouth to Trent's ear as he whispered, "I wouldn't be averse to some company in the shower." Another kiss, this to the curve of Trent's ear. "Just sayin'."

"Jericho, forge your uncle's signature if we're not out of the shower by the time pizza gets here."

Jericho's laughter chased Trent up the hallway, close on the heels of a Jacob already shedding clothes, shirt and socks flying in opposite directions.

Jericho

Shaking his head, Jericho walked directly to the living room couch where he'd left the remote for the TV, using the device to dramatically increase the volume. He'd quickly learned that when his uncles had that look on their faces and disappeared together, he really didn't want to hear any of the noises that came from their bedroom.

Perching on the edge of the couch cushions, he stared at the TV without seeing the comedic antics on the screen. The remote clattered against the table as he set it down, his hand trembling uncontrollably.

The memory of Trent's voice echoed through his head, a loop of pain and panic that grew in volume until it drowned out anything else around him.

"I want to be able to touch you, to kiss you. To damn well hold your hand if I want to."

Jericho remembered walking with them through the mall in Knoxville, a town not unlike Memphis. Even after only a narrow introduction to the affection and love shared between the two men, he'd easily picked up on the changes when they were in public. Standing close, but not too close. Shoulders brushing, but no arms around waists. Backs of fingers in a slight, grazing caress, but none of the finger-twined handholding he knew was so much a part of who they were. No kissing, no touching, no expressions of love, no endearingly saccharine statements of devotion from either of them.

It was wrong.

The local grocery store a few days ago was a better representation of what he knew his uncles should be like in public, an only slightly dialed-back version of their private selves. Trent leaned over a vegetable display, and when he stood, Jake was there, his arm wrapping around Trent's chest, pulling the bigger man firmly against him as they discussed the merits of organic versus hydroponic tomatoes. Trent turned his head to rest against Jake's shoulder on the cereal aisle, asking for someone to help select something, crying out about how all the decisions were so tedious. Being enough of himself to relax Jake and Jericho, no one on the alert for possible witnesses, because it didn't matter here.

In only the couple of weeks he'd spent here in San Diego, Jericho had seen dozens upon dozens of real-life examples of the motto "love is love," and he'd quickly grown accustomed to the openness of same-sex couples.

If they moved back to Memphis, Trent and Jake would lose that.

If they move us back there, I'll never have that.

Sure, Jake's family was welcoming, but even in his most generous dreams, Jericho couldn't imagine Memphis being much different from Knoxville, and he knew firsthand how anti-gay the greater populous there was. People were more like Frank than folks wanted to believe.

And now Trent was seeing just what a mistake it would be. *Where does that leave me?* They weren't talking about it because of him, and having to take on the burden of Jericho, but it surely played a factor in the eventual decision. Trent was already talking about moving schools again, and Jericho hadn't even started here in California yet.

A commercial blasted from the TV speakers, and he stared at the screen, watching as frantic faces shouted at the camera. Some legal proposal was up for vote, and this was one of a dozen commercials he'd seen for it so far. White signs, black letters, open mouths, screaming voices—but at least it was being talked about here. In Knoxville...in Tennessee, as far as he knew, there'd been no positive discussion about gays living as equals, only how the Christian sect could break federal law allowing it.

Memories of Frank's voice crept in around the edges of his mind. The hurtful, hateful words, the names, the disgusted tone. How it felt to be belittled, mocked and made to believe his existence was wrong.

Jericho was still focused on the TV minutes later when a half-dressed Jake startled him by striding through the room, breaking his gaze. "Jericho, didn't you hear the doorbell?" Jake opened the door, and there stood a pizza delivery guy, an annoyed expression on his face as Jake did what he always did, smiled and smoothed it over. Door closed, world shut outside again, Jake took the box into the kitchen. Jericho expected him to disappear back up the hallway and startled when the man settled onto the couch next to where Jericho sat.

Wordlessly, Jake stretched out his arm in invitation and Jericho accepted, sinking sideways against him until Jake held him firmly. The strength and constant caring of this man shouldn't still be a surprise, not when it was modeled every day. A few minutes later, Trent wandered out, the damp hair and bemused expression on his face telling Jericho at least his inattentiveness hadn't cost his uncle too much of the alone time with Jake.

Trent sank into the cushions on Jericho's other side, lifted the cast onto his knee, and slipped his arm around Jericho, leaning in so Jericho was sandwiched between these two men he was coming to understand loved him. A family he'd needed for so long, given to him by tragedy. *Silver linings*.

"I love you guys."

"We love you, too, sweet baby boy." Trent shifted, and Jericho knew he was sharing a look with Jake over his head. "Wanna tell us what's going on in that head of yours?"

"I was just thinking." Holding his peace was the better choice here, not delving into the maelstrom of thoughts and fears that had rocked him to his core.

"Uh-huh. And we were showering together to conserve water." Jericho snorted at Jake's description, then laughed aloud when Trent's hand moved and he heard a smacking sound. "Don't hit me, babe."

"Don't say things like that. We're like parents now, and it's damaging to children's psyche to know their parents do *it*." Trent hugged Jericho tight again. "I'm sorry for Jakey, Jericho. Don't hold his lack of understanding against him."

"Pretty sure Jericho knows we do *it*, Trentie." Jake's gruff voice was strained with laughter. "Jericho, does it bother you to know your uncles are sexually active?"

Jericho had squeezed his eyes shut when the two of them started, trying to keep from laughing out loud. Into the dark, he admitted, "Uh, kinda? It's a little weird, to be honest."

"See?" Trent's cry was loud and anguished, and it nearly broke Jericho's control.

"But does it squidge you out?" Jake was shaking with laughter now, his deep chuckles breaking through in-between words.

"A little?" Jericho lost control when Trent made another anguished sound and burst into laughter. "Not really, Uncle Trent. It's okay. I'm not scarred forever or anything. It's all good, okay? You shouldn't have to worry about being yourselves in your own home."

"It's your home, too, Jericho. If it bothered you, we'd find a way to respect that." Jake's tone was his firm, do-not-argue-with-me one, and Jericho nodded. "But it's good to know I can mack on my husband in the kitchen without you squidging out over it."

"You cannot mack on me." Trent turned loose of Jericho and shifted so he faced the two of them on the couch, a look of horror on his face. "That's my thing. You don't get that. I mack on you, honeybuns. You kiss me tenderly."

Jericho smiled at Trent, glad to see an amused expression in return. *Might as well ask the questions now.*

"What happens if you move to Memphis? How does that work when you're in stores and stuff? Or at the movies? Eating dinner?"

"When *we* move to Memphis." Jericho didn't miss Jake's emphasis, and he ducked his head with a nod as he sat back so he could look between his uncles. "We'll live in a community that's more progressive. Just like we do here. Jericho, just because you don't see it around here doesn't mean prejudice doesn't exist." Jake pointed to the TV, where another political ad was playing. "It's everywhere. There are no safe spaces for gays and queers. And as much as the LGBTQ community wants things to move forwards more rapidly, it'll only go as fast as people are willing to change their thinking. There are several different areas in Memphis that are welcoming, and Conner's looking into those school districts for us. We want to make certain the transition will be as comfortable as we can make it for you, too. Germantown is the leading candidate, in case you wanted to look it up and check it out for yourself. It's a fact of life for us, Jericho." Jake shook his head and reached for Trent, who took his hand. Jericho watched as their fingers did that natural thing, falling into place as if made for each other. "I heard someone describe the most profound difference between a hetero couple's public affection and a gay couple's. For us, it is always an act of courage, because every time we hold hands or kiss, or even walk with arms around the other, we know in our gut that we're courting physical danger. We quickly learn how to gauge a room, a street, a crowd. I hate it, but it's something you'll figure out, too. All we can do is mitigate the challenges as best we can."

"And love each other always." Trent's eyes were misty, lashes clumped together as he stared at Jake. "Right, hunka-hunka?"

"Always." In Jake's voice, Jericho heard determination and courage, and he was so glad to have witnessed this moment between these two men. *My role models.*

Jericho's phone buzzed loudly in his pocket, and Trent glanced down at him, the soft smile still in place. "Let's eat pizza before it gets too cold. Come on, honeybuns. Jericho has a hot date with a text message."

Jake rolled his eyes at Jericho and made as if to stand up, then paused. "You okay, kiddo?" Jericho nodded quickly. "No, are you okay, kiddo?"

"Yeah, Uncle Jake. I'm okay. This…helped, if you can believe it."

"Oh, I believe it. I'm *always* helpful. Jacob, why aren't there any clean plates?" Trent's voice drifted back from the kitchen, where he banged one cabinet door closed after another. "Where are all the clean plates?"

"Just use paper." Jake stood and pointed the remote to the TV, changing the channel to show a baseball game. "Don't get so stuck in your own head, Jericho. No question's off-limits. You can always ask anything."

"Except what comes in the plain, brown paper packages. Those are waaaay off-limits." Trent was laughing. "Oh, plates. Found 'em. I thought you were going to unload the dishwasher, Jakey?"

"Babe."

Jericho laughed at the anticipatory expression on Jake's face when he uttered the single word, then was able to see the soft, pleased look as he got what he wanted.

"Not a 'babe' situation, honeybuns."

Jake glanced down and muttered, "Oh, he's wrong. It's always a 'babe' situation." Jake paused again, then glanced at the phone Jericho had taken out, Jordan's name on the plethora of texts just like Trent had expected. "Be good to Jordan. He's one of the decent ones." With that, Jake strode around the couch and into the kitchen, calling out another amused, "Babe."

Maybe it'll be okay. Jericho watched the reflections of his uncles in the window glass, seeing Jake move closer, the two blurred outlines merging for a long minute before separating.

Maybe.

♥ ♥ ♥

Trent

"How's the arm feel? Is it weird?" They were on their way home from visiting the doctor, and Trent carefully watched traffic as he drove, eyes on the cars ahead of and beside him. Jericho sat in the passenger seat, and from the corner of his eye, Trent saw him moving and stretching the arm so recently released from the imprisonment of the cast. Said cast was in the back seat, the stinky carcass encased in plastic for now. The doctor had been amused at Jericho's insistence on keeping it, until Trent had explained the signatures. Then the man had explained what they could do to lessen the smell so the trip souvenir could be displayed however Jericho wanted.

Even Jericho had been surprised at the smell, and at how his arm looked coming out of the cast after almost six weeks. The first thing the doc had done was hand Jericho a dampened cloth, telling him to "Scratch that itch that's been making you crazy. Gently now." Trent had tried not to laugh, but Jericho's eyes had rolled back in his head as he scraped the cloth along his arm, and the almost orgasmic expression was comical.

After that, the visit had gone quickly, the doctor asking empathetic questions, having clearly read the history Trent had been so persistent in providing. At the end, Trent had been walking up the hallway to pay at the window when he'd overheard an exchange between the doctor and Jericho that had both hurt his heart and helped heal it all at once.

"Your uncle seems nice. I'm sorry for your loss, but you could have landed in a very different spot, so it's good that when you needed him, he's been there for you." The doctor's murmur hadn't been for Trent, but he'd appreciated the sentiment.

It was Jericho's response that had torn Trent up. "My uncles." There'd been a pause, then Jericho continued, "Uncle Trent is married to Uncle Jake. I know I'm lucky to have them. They dropped everything and came for me, made it so I won't ever be alone again. He's more than just nice. Uncle Trent is everything."

Trent's phone rang, interrupting the memory, and he thumbed the control on the steering wheel, answering with a "Trent Conway," in case it was a client. Jericho knew the drill and stayed silent on his side of the car.

"Mr. Conway, this is Nadine from the Evergrowing Family Clinic." Trent froze for a long moment, then jerked back into movement, belatedly jamming on the brakes just in time to avoid rear-ending the vehicle in front of him as traffic stopped for a red light. "Is now a good time?"

"Uh, yes. No. I don't know." *No, it's not a good time.* This was the fertility and surrogacy clinic calling, and Trent definitely couldn't do this now, not driving and not without Jacob. "Not really. I'm in traffic. Can I call back in fifteen minutes or so? It'll take me that long to get home and get my husband on the phone, too. Do I need to get my husband on the phone? Is this bad news? It's bad news, isn't it? I should just take the call now."

"Uncle Trent, the light's green." Trent glanced at Jericho and then out at the street, seeing the vehicles in front of him had somehow disappeared.

"Oh, sh-rap."

The woman on the phone laughed softly, and Trent immediately tried to analyze the laughter. Was it at his abbreviated swearing or was it about him being so distracted he didn't realize the light had changed? Was it in judgment of his ability to parent a child? *If they could see us with Jericho, they'd realize we have this parenting thing in control*. "Calling back is fine, Mr. Conway. You have the number?"

Trent stared at the display, trying to memorize the number showing there. "Yeah, I think so."

"Okay then, I'll wait for your call."

"Wait, what was your name again?" Panic set in, because what if he called and talked to the wrong person and somehow made a life-altering decision for a different couple.

"Nadine. It's Nadine, Mr. Conway. And it's not bad news. Just breathe, get your husband on the phone, and call me back. I'll talk to you soon."

The call disconnected, and the car was filled with the overly peppy J-pop Jericho claimed to like today. Trent stared through the windshield, turned on his blinker, and eased around a corner, pulling the car to a stop along the curb.

"Holy shit." He fumbled with the steering wheel, unable to feel the buttons that would disconnect the phone from the car's system.

Ringing filled the car and he panicked, believing he'd called Nadine back prematurely. He shoved the gearshift all the way up and threw open his door. He was still trying to climb out of the vehicle while buckled in when he heard Jericho's quavering voice, "Uncle Jake. Something's wrong with Uncle Trent."

Then Jacob's voice was there, all around him, smothering the fear that had been driving Trent from the car. "What's wrong, Jericho? Trent? Trentie? Babe, you there?"

"Yeah." He sounded like a dying frog, croaking out his last. "Yeah, Jakey. Jakey, Jakey. I'm here."

"What's wrong?" A car horn drowned out Jacob's voice, and Trent yanked at the door, slamming it closed, shutting himself in with the welcome sound of Jacob. "Babe?"

"He got a call from someplace called the Evergrowing Family Clinic. A lady named Nadine. He just started freaking out."

Thank God Jericho could still talk, because Trent wasn't capable right now.

"Trent, the clinic called? What'd they say?"

Trent turned to look at Jericho. The boy was plastered against the door, face paler than his arm, which hadn't seen the sun in a month and a half. Trent opened his mouth, then closed it. Opened, and closed.

"She said it wasn't bad news. Uncle Trent told her he was going to get you on the phone and call them back." Jericho shook his head, staring at Trent. "Who are they, Uncle Jake?"

"It's the agency that handles surrogacy. She said she had news?"

"Yeah." Trent's voice returned, finally. "Yeah, she's got news. Why does she have news, Jakey? I don't understand."

"You turned in our application, babe. Remember the picnic we didn't go to? It's been months, and I don't know why she's calling now, but we'll figure it out together. Are you okay now? Can you drive?" Jacob didn't wait for him to respond, continuing on in a take-charge tone that did more to settle Trent's nerves than he'd ever admit to his husband. "Where are you? I'll come get you. You're not okay to drive."

"I'm okay." Even Trent didn't believe his statement, and he felt a moment of amusement when he saw Jericho's massive eye roll in response. "Okay, maybe I'm not there yet, but I'm better. Just hearing you makes it better, Jakey. I'll pull it together. Promise. We'll be home in a few minutes. It just took me by surprise."

"Surprise, so that's what you call it?"

Jericho's *sotto voce* mutter had been the go-signal for Trent's laughter, and that sound must have convinced Jacob, because he grudgingly gave permission for Trent to continue on their way.

"Come home to me."

It was closer to thirty minutes before they returned Nadine's call, not fifteen, but the delay didn't change the news.

They'd been approved for the program, and a surrogate had already selected them.

Jericho

Lying on top of the covers on his bed, Jericho tried hard not to listen to the conversation from the kitchen. But, even through his closed door, there was no mistaking the excitement and fear in both men's voices as they again talked about the call with the clinic.

"I know we can, but should we?" Trent's voice carried best, his expressive tone filled with both anxiety and excitement. "Right now? We're not even going to be here this time next year. We'll be in Memphis. Why would the surrogate say yes to that?"

Jake's words were spoken with clarity and sincerity, stating what he thought and felt without downplaying Trent's worries. It was a balancing act Jericho had watched him demonstrate masterfully throughout the weeks he'd known them, and tonight when the emotions were so high, he'd been in awe of how Jake had been able to hold it together in the face of Trent's doubts and fears. "Why wouldn't she? Not every couple is involved in the pregnancy to a great extent. I know Cooper and Marie were with Jaime, but that's not a gold standard. If we're here or there, in Memphis, it doesn't change our commitment or support. If we're in this, then we'll be in it a hundred percent, no matter if it's physically at the sonogram or via video chat."

"But we'd miss out on so much." Trent's voice had softened, become less strident, and Jericho hoped it meant his uncle was coming to terms with whatever drove his anxiety.

"No, babe." Jake's tone dipped lower, and the rest of what he said was lost to the distance, a muffled mumble that still conveyed reassurance and trust.

Jericho stared up at the ceiling, running his hand up and down the arm that had been broken. The sensation was still novel, weird. Glancing down, he noted again how different it looked. White and withered, so much smaller than the other one. He tightened his fist as hard as he could, holding it until the muscles shook with the strain, and then released it with a huff of air. It didn't hurt, not exactly, but it didn't feel right, either.

His phone buzzed on the nightstand next to the bed, and he rolled over, marveling at how much easier it was to maneuver just that much without the cast. He looked at the screen, and with a grin, pushed up in bed and grabbed the phone, swiping to answer the video call.

"Hey, Nate." He started talking before the video had fully resolved. "Got my cast off today and man, it feels weird. Check it out." Holding the phone away from his body, he scanned up and down his arm. "Look how freakish it is. All tiny and stuff."

Turning the phone back to his face, he froze, his wide smile slowly fading.

Jordan was grinning at him from the phone.

Jordan, whom he'd been trying unsuccessfully to ignore, not wanting to hear another rendition of "I'm sorry" from the man who featured nightly in Jericho's dreams.

Jordan who was hot as sin, good as the day was long, and—straight as an arrow.

"Hey." Jericho hated how stilted he sounded, the three-letter word coming out garbled somehow, like his lips and tongue didn't work right while barely looking at Jordan's face. Imagine if he had to actually talk to him. In person. *I'd forget to breathe or something. Fall dead at his feet.* "I'm not dead." *Oh, God. Kill me now.* "I mean, not that it was an option or anything." No, the better option would be to disconnect the call and hide under the covers. Where his dreams happened. Every single night. "What are you doing on my phone?" *On my phone while I'm in bed. Oh, God. I don't have pants on and I showed him my arm. Did he see my underwear? Oh, God.*

"Hi, Jericho." Jordan's voice was soft, rolling through the video like an impossible wave of caramel-smooth charm. "You weren't answering my texts or calls, so I got Nate to let me use his phone to call you. I hope you don't mind." *Mind? Of course I don't mind. I'm just going to die now.* "I mean..." Jordan glanced away, then back to the camera, looking straight at Jericho. "Of course you mind. If you didn't mind, you would have picked up at least once, right? But I—" Jordan's head dipped to the side and he glared at something off camera. Raising his voice, he called, "Nate, get away from the door. I can hear you breathing, bud. Come on. Give a man some privacy."

"Nate's not there with you?" Jericho didn't know if that raised or lowered the insane factor of this call. He'd assumed Nate had called and Jordan had somehow commandeered the phone away. "Are you in the bathroom?" If he'd locked himself into the bathroom alone to make the call, things went from insane to insanely weird. *And this was plenty weird to start with.* "By yourself?"

"Yeah, by myself." Jordan's brows drew together in an endearing expression of confusion. *He even scowls cutely. I'm dead.* "Why would I want anyone with me when we're talking?"

"I don't know. He's your friend." Jericho stopped himself there, trapping the "not me" part of what he'd been thinking. "You call him bud. That's cute." *Abort! Straight guys don't like to be called cute.* "I mean, friendly. That's friendly."

"Jericho, can you let me talk for a minute?" One corner of Jordan's mouth lifted, a dimple on that cheek winking into existence and immediately becoming the only thing Jericho could focus on. "I'll take your silence as agreement for now." A pause, then Jordan's voice dipped an octave, coming out growly like Jake's did when he was teasing Uncle Trent. "But only for this. I'll need affirmative consent for other things." Jericho made an embarrassing squeaking sound and Jordan blinked, the dimple disappearing. Jericho decided to mourn it later; he needed to focus right now. "I call and text because I want to get to know you better. I know it won't be long until you guys are here in Memphis, but I don't want to wait, Jericho. I just—" The camera jostled, and Jordan ran a hand through his thick hair, making Jericho wonder immediately if it was as soft as it seemed. "I just want to talk to you, but you keep ghosting me. Jacob told me to wait—"

"You talked to Uncle Jake about me?" Jericho pulled his legs up, folding his arm across them and transferring the phone to that hand. "Why would you do that?"

"I don't know." Jordan looked baffled. "Because you're cute and I wanted to make sure you were okay. I know I'm older, but—"

"Three years isn't that much older. I'll be sixteen in a couple of months." Jericho's eyes widened as he realized how that sounded. "I mean, you and Nate are friends, and he's a lot younger than you are."

"It's nearly four years, but you're right, it's not that much older." The smile was back, and Jericho watched with held breath until Jordan's lips curved enough to waken that dimple. *Oh God.* "But Jericho, Nate and I are just friends. He's a cool guy who understands a lot about me. We've been buds for a long time. And we're friends, yeah. But we're *just* friends." Jordan blinked, and Jericho saw it in slow motion, the brilliance of his blue eyes disappearing for an instant, then back and directed on him, Jordan's full focus aimed his way. The smile changed, turning a tiny bit sly, something Jericho would have killed to experience in person. "I want to get to know you a different way."

"Different?" Jericho closed his eyes instead of rolling them at himself. *Oh, different? I speak words. Yuk, yuk, yuk. God.* "What does that mean, Jordan?"

"Look at me and ask that again." Jericho opened his eyes and stared; Jordan's gaze still locked on him through the camera almost felt like a touch across his skin. "Ask me, Jericho. I'm not afraid to tell you exactly what it means."

"You're straight." The numero uno reason he'd been not answering the calls. "I've read about boys crushing on their straight friends. It never ends well."

"What?" Jordan's laughter hurt, physical pain lashing across Jericho until he wanted to drop the phone and smash it, pulverize it underfoot until it was shards of nothingness. "No, Jericho, I assure you, I am not straight."

Pounding in the background had Jordan's head whipping to the side, and he snarled—*even his snarl is handsome*—at the door. "Not *now*, Nate."

"Okay." Nate's voice sounded deflated and sad, and Jericho saw Jordan's expression change. "I'll just go wait in my room. Where you and I will be in a few minutes. Alone. Nothing to see here, Jericho." By the end of Nate's little speech, Jordan's face had turned red, and instead of looking at the camera, he was glancing around. It seemed like he was doing anything to avoid looking at Jericho.

"Jordan." Jericho waited, holding his breath until Jordan looked up, uncertainty written on his expression. "Nate's a little turd sometimes."

"He is." Shaking his head, Jordan snorted. "Love the turd, though. He's like a brother to me." As Jordan stared into the camera again, his voice did that dip thing when he spoke. "He's nothing like you."

"You're…you're not straight?" Jericho needed confirmation. Again. Certainty that his mind wasn't making him hear what he wanted instead of what was said. "Really?"

"Really. I'm gay."

Jericho stared at him for a moment, sweat breaking out across his neck at the idea of saying those words aloud again. For only the third time ever. "I'm…Jordan, I'm gay, too." His breath was coming in great whoops, like there wasn't enough oxygen in the room. He sucked air in and in, only blowing out enough to make that switch to drawing it in again. Things started going out of focus, dark and sparkly at the edges, and he remembered suddenly when he'd passed out in the hospital the night before his mother died.

"*Jericho.*" Jordan's voice was filled with concern, shouting Jericho's name over and over until Jericho looked at him. "Jericho, are you okay?" He nodded, not willing to trust his voice. "Is that the first time you've told anyone?"

"No." He shook his head, surprised he'd gotten even the one word out through his clogged throat. Another attempt at speaking wasn't as successful, and he waved his hand dismissively, covering his eyes when Jordan angled closer to the camera to try and peer into his face.

"It's okay. I got you." Jordan's voice was quiet, soothing. Seeming to instinctively realize Jericho couldn't continue right now, Jordan quietly filled the silence that threatened between them. The topics varied as he moved from one to another, talking about inconsequential things like the weather and classes, his car, his sister, Nate and Matt, or Coach and Jaime. It took a while, but finally Jericho felt like he could say what he needed to without fainting or puking, both of which had been in question earlier.

"Jordan?" The blue eyes hadn't left him, but the stare intensified when Jericho called his name into a brief break between stories. "You aren't the first. I told Uncle Jake and Uncle Trent before we left Knoxville."

"But outside of them, I'm the first?" Jericho nodded. Jordan's chin lifted, and a muscle jumped in his jaw. "In that case, I'm honored you trusted me, Jericho. Honored."

"It's not... It shouldn't be such a big deal."

"Shouldn't be, I'll give you that. But it is. The reality is, saying the words is a big, big deal, no matter when or where it happens. I'm glad, so damn glad you felt safe with me."

"But you knew, right? You wouldn't have said the things you did without knowing. How did you know?" If Jericho could understand how Jordan had decided Jericho's sexual orientation was complementary to his own, then maybe Jericho could figure out other people easier. Sometimes, as with Trent who wore it boldly in his every expression, it was clear as day. But someone like Jake even? Jericho had watched men and women alike give his uncle considering glances when they were out shopping.

"I hoped." Jordan's eyelashes dropped as he offered what felt like a whispered confession. "I hoped, Jericho. But I didn't know."

With more confidence than he felt, Jericho said, "You do now."

Jordan's smile activated both dimples this time.

Jericho was pretty certain death by dimples was a thing.

Chapter Ten
Trent

Flinging himself into the plastic torture device that airlines deigned to call a seat in the gate waiting area, Trent rolled his head to the side to see Jacob grinning at him. "What?"

"I don't know why you insist on drinking coffee on mornings when we're traveling. You always freak out about having to pee on the plane, so you make a dozen trips to the bathroom as if that'll make your bladder work faster." Jacob shrugged. "It's cute."

Laughter from his other side made Trent glance over his shoulder. Jericho was folded into a seat similar to the one Trent sat in, but he looked entirely too comfortable for it to be real. "Don't laugh at your elders. I know you're sixteen now, but I'm still older than you."

"Pretty sure you're always going to be older than me, Uncle Trent." Jericho flashed a grin at him to soften the words, then finished up with a killer line. "You're cool for an old guy."

"Gah, why do I like you again?" Trent huffed out a breath, looking up to scan the departures list. Still twenty minutes before they boarded.

"Not sure you do." When Trent looked back at Jericho, he was frowning down at the phone in his hand. He'd tap on the screen in a flurry of movements, then make a repetitive motion Trent was pretty sure equaled backspacing over what he'd just written. Then Jericho did the whole cycle again.

"I lub joo." Trent pushed out his bottom lip, which got him a distracted grin before Jericho was totally focused on the phone again. "Who are you texting? Nate?"

"No, not Nate." Jericho's tongue appeared in the corner of his mouth; then he bit his bottom lip. "I lub joo, too."

"Leave the boy alone, Trent. He's busy." Jacob's hand landed on Trent's thigh, fingers sliding down the inside until he could trace along the seam with a fingertip. "Give him a break."

On cue, as he had a dozen times since getting the cast off, Jericho held up the arm that had been broken, and without looking around, teased, "No thanks, already had one."

In the couple of weeks since getting the cast off, he'd worked diligently on the exercises assigned by the doctor, and it was showing. The arm looked more like its counterpart. One of a thousand reasons to give thanks that Jericho hadn't suffered any lasting harm from the events in Knoxville.

Jericho sucked in a breath then tapped the phone, dropping it into his lap with a sigh. Jacob reached across Trent and neatly plucked it up, ignoring Jericho's screeching response.

"That's it? That took you ten minutes to type out and send?" Jacob angled the phone so Trent could see the screen. Sure enough, it was a text string with Jordan, and the most recent one from Jericho said simply: **That's cool**. Jacob held the phone out, letting Jericho snatch it back. "Lame-o. You gotta step your game up, son. Need to work on those lines."

Jericho stared at him, mouth slack. His breath hitched as water gathered in his eyes.

Jacob leaned forwards, holding a conciliatory hand out. "Jericho, I didn't mean anything by—"

"You called me son. Again."

Trent stilled at the quietly spoken words, which had been filled with terrible pain. Not only were they taking the boy back to Tennessee, even if it was the far end of the state from where everything had happened, now Jacob had stirred up something.

"It's how I think of you." Jacob's words were so gentle, as persistently tender as he was when talking to Nate or Matt, or even Trent when he felt unsure. Honesty was inherent in Jacob's very nature. He didn't flinch from what he saw as the truth. "If you don't like it, I'll do my best to remember that."

"I didn't say that." Jericho looked at Trent, and the questions in his eyes didn't need to be spoken. They were clear and present and needed an answer now. "I didn't say that at all."

"We both think of you as a son. I understand you haven't known us for long." Trent swallowed, terrified now that the gate attendants would call for boarding and this conversation wouldn't be finished. It needed to be said; Jericho deserved to know how much they loved him. "But I—we love you. You're stuck with us, all your days. You're our family, not because I'm your uncle, but because we want you. We want you with us, and we hope you want us too."

Blinking fast, Jericho nodded, then dropped his gaze to the phone. After a long, anguished pause, Jericho sniffed and quietly asked, "Uncle Jakey, can you teach me some better lines? I don't want Jordan to think he's not worth the effort. He is." The phone buzzed and Jericho nearly dropped it in his haste to position the screen where he could read it. The sigh he released carried so much tension Trent could see the boy's shoulders drop two inches. "That teaching you mentioned? Now would be good."

Jacob moved to the other side of Jericho, angling his head towards the boy, and Trent drew a silent breath. He knew they hadn't gotten to anything hard yet, but if Jericho was willing to vocalize things like he just had, maybe they'd come out the other end doing a little bit of all right.

Jericho

Head down, Jericho studied the laces in his new shoes, methodically tracing the lines across and through the eyelet holes, and then across again. They were even, left and right shoes laced in opposite directions, and nothing was twisted or out of sorts.

Jericho had no other excuses to stay in the bedroom.

Nate's bed was neatly made, as was the one Jericho had slept in. Far more comfortable now than he'd been the first time he'd stayed in this room, he had stayed up with Nate for hours last night, talking about a dozen topics. Everything Jericho could think or ask about, Nate either knew tons more than he did and had a distinct opinion on or would immediately dive into research mode, digging to find out what intrigued Jericho.

The whole family was downstairs in the kitchen or out in the backyard. Arriving at the Thompson house yesterday afternoon, following Jericho's first airplane ride— something that was equal parts thrilling and terrifying— he'd been swamped with attention and affection. Jaime, Nate, and Matt had all approached with arms wide, and even Connor had slipped in a sideways hug. There'd been cake and ice cream, even as Jaime waved off his thanks, telling him that the real celebration would be happening later.

Later, as in today.

They'd just been waiting on Connor's family to arrive. His parents from somewhere in Arkansas, and his brother, sister-in-law, and two nephews from a house not far from here.

And Jordan, who'd finished his summer semester classes two days ago and driven all night to get home. He'd been stuck at a family dinner last night, but every message and conversation Jericho'd had with him in the past couple of days had ended the same. Jordan promising to be here.

Jericho shook himself and blew out a nervous breath. He tugged at the cuffs of his shirtsleeves, second-guessing his decision to wear long sleeves, even if the shirt was lightweight. The weather was typical late summer in Memphis, and the backyard would be sweltering. But his arm still looked weird, and if it were on display, he'd feel self-conscious.

"Jesus." He scrubbed his sweaty hands on the legs of jeans, then shoved his fingers through his hair, digging deep into his scalp as he pulled his head forwards. He and Jordan video chatted every chance they had; Jericho didn't know why he was so nervous. "This is stupid."

The door clicked, and he looked up, hands frozen in his hair as he watched Jordan peer tentatively through the slowly widening gap. "Hey."

There had been no way for a phone or computer to effectively replicate the resonance in Jordan's deep voice, and Jericho suddenly hated the technology for the lack. He should have had at least a fighting chance to desensitize himself to the sounds, should have had a defense against how attractive just that one word was, when said in Jordan's voice.

He realized he was staring at the man like an idiot.

Suddenly aware he probably looked like that crazy picture of Einstein with his hair all over the place, Jericho yanked his hands away from his head, pulling out multiple strands of hair. He frantically patted and smoothed at his hair, trying to straighten something he couldn't even see.

From Jordan's concerned expression as he stepped into the bedroom and closed the door behind him—*closed the door*—Jericho wasn't sure if he should run away, puke, or do a combination of both.

"I...uh. I wanted to wish you a happy birthday." Jordan took a step towards him, Jericho staring up at him, a hundred percent sure he looked even more like a madman with his mouth gaping open. "In private."

Jericho made to stand, but a hand on his shoulder kept him in place as Jordan crouched in front of him. His other hand was on Jericho's knee, a furnace branding his skin through his jeans, and a location that was both entirely too close to a delicate part of his anatomy and simultaneously too far away.

His mind had short-circuited. That was the only explanation for the buzzing in his ears and how his skin hummed, overworked lungs failing in their efforts to take in enough air to keep him upright.

Jordan pushed closer, one knee on the floor as he rose in front of Jericho. His position on the bed and Jordan's kneeling in front of him put them at about the same height. Jordan's head tilted to the side, those bottomless blue eyes skimming across Jericho's face. The hand on his shoulder disappeared just before there was a welcome heat against the side of his face. When he leaned into that touch, he saw Jordan's lips part slightly. Coral colored and puffy, as if he'd been biting at them, those lips took up all of Jericho's attention.

"So…uh." Jordan moved closer, his hand on Jericho's cheek a steadying touch. "Happy birthday, Jericho."

The kiss started as a tender brush of Jordan's lips against his. Bristles of a midday scruff prickled the skin around Jericho's mouth, and his eyes closed as he lost himself in the sensation. Strength, heat, and softness were followed by a heavier press against his mouth—each facet was mesmerizing. More scruff dusted against the pad of his thumb, which was Jericho's first inkling that his hands hadn't stayed in his lap, and he used the unexpected access to familiarize himself with the contours of Jordan's jaw and throat. That thick hair was just as soft as he'd hoped, and he tried to split his attention between the glorious things happening with the kiss and this chance to explore Jordan through touch.

Jordan pulled back, and Jericho knew he'd be embarrassed later for the soft whimper that crept up his throat following that retreat. With their foreheads pressed together, Jordan's hands had come to rest on both sides of his face, and Jericho gripped the strong wrists to keep them exactly there, his head cradled in Jordan's strong hold. So close were their mouths, the very breath they took was shared, gusts of heated air passing back and forth between them. Ragged exhales and shuddering inhales were his first clue that Jordan was just as affected as Jericho.

Jericho's mind was slowly rebooting, and he was suddenly aware that he hadn't spoken since Jordan had stepped into the room. He tried to force out a word, something, but all that came out was an airy, whispered, "Hey."

"God, I've wanted to do that for so long." Jordan's whisper was another example of how poorly technology could replicate the action a person's sounds created, because if he'd been on the phone, there'd be no way for Jericho to have known how Jordan trembled as he spoke. "Jericho." Jordan pulled back and Jericho blinked, letting his eyes accustom to the light. It took a moment to focus on Jordan's face, but when he did, that single look was worth everything. Tender and caring, the expression was no longer tentative, but astonished. "You're so gorgeous."

Jericho had never felt so cherished in his life. There was no other word for the feeling ricocheting through him. Held like this, kissed like that, stripped bare by Jordan's gaze right now—cherished.

"Jordan, I've never—"

A finger against his lips was a gentle but effective shush, so Jericho stopped talking and watched as Jordan's gaze again tracked across his face. "It's your birthday, Jericho. All you have to be today is happy." Jordan's grip tightened on Jericho's face, holding him steady as they stared at each other. "Everything else can wait."

The doorknob rattled; then there were three soft knocks followed by Nate's voice. "Five-second warning. Put away anything that might harm my delicate, youthful psyche." Jordan's lips curled in a smile, and Jericho watched as both dimples came out to play. He saw Jordan's lips move but didn't hear anything, didn't know when Nate came into the room, because those dimples were right there in front of him. Jericho darted forwards to press a kiss against one, running his thumb across the other.

He pulled back and looked up into Jordan's face, which wore an expression of stunned pleasure. "Dimples," he said, as if that explained everything going through his head at that moment.

"Oh man, is this going to be a thing now?" Jericho looked over at Nate, who was talking through his broad grin. He fluttered his eyelashes, clasped his hands to his chest, and sighed, "My cousin and my best buddy?"

Jordan shifted to the side, gaze staying on Jericho's face, as if he couldn't get his fill of looking. "Yeah, it is. So you're going to have to get used to it, bud."

In his normal voice, Nate cautioned them, "Just don't let Uncle Trent catch you."

"Don't let Uncle Trent catch you doing what?" Trent pushed past the door Nate had left ajar, and Jericho was suddenly aware he had hold of Jordan's shirt with one fist, the other hand still propped on his neck. Jordan had one hand around his waist, holding Jericho against him as best he could while Jericho still sat on the bed. "Jordie, are you mackin' on my nephew? Gonna have to put a halt to it. Sorry." Jericho's dismay must have been plain, because Trent laughed softly. "For now at least. It's time for cake and ice cream, and I was dispatched to bring the missing guest of honor to his own party."

Jericho looked at each face in turn, leaving Jordan for last, not surprised when he found that the expression of love and affection he'd seen on the other two people in the room was slightly different from the one Jordan was giving him.

Cherished.

❤ ❤ ❤

Trent

"Will you just get in the car?" Trent stared over the top of the rental at Jacob, who'd bent to look at something alongside the driveway. Jacob straightened and looked at him, the expression on his face puzzled. "Puleeze? Before I'm eighty and dying of waiting over here?"

"We're just going to the grocery store." Jacob moved to the car and hesitated. "We are just going to the grocery store, right?"

"If you don't get in the car, we'll be going to the morgue." Trent's mutter probably didn't hold as much venom as he intended, because as he was folding into the car, he knocked the top of his head against the doorframe. "Oh my God, even the car's trying to kill me." Head cradled in his hands, he leaned against the steering wheel, hoping the pain would ease any moment.

"Babe." Jacob was right next to Trent, gently pulling his hands away from his head. "Let me see."

"Is it bleeding? It's bleeding, isn't it." Jacob's fingers traced across Trent's forehead, and he winced, pulling away. "Ow. Stop it."

"You're not bleeding." Pressure on the side of his head pulled him towards Jacob, and Trent relaxed against Jacob's chest, the arms around him for comfort not so much support, but it still felt good to be held. "Want me to drive?"

"Yes." Trent was pouting and knew it, but he didn't care. His head hurt.

A few minutes later, Trent was installed in the passenger seat, Jacob behind the wheel, and they were at the intersection that led out of the community where Jaime and Connor lived.

Jacob turned and shot him a sly smile. "Sooooo. Is 'grocery store' code for me getting plowed in the back seat?"

"No." Trent chuckled, amused in spite of himself. "It's code for the actual grocery store."

"That's less fun than it could be." Jacob touched the navigation screen, and within seconds, the atonal voice was providing directions to the nearest shopping center. "You're here. I'm here. We're here together. Without Jericho or Nate or Matt. Just you and me."

"And what are we doing?" Trent glanced out the window at the landscaped yards leading up to immaculate homes.

"We're goin' shoppin'." Jacob's overly enthusiastic response made Trent laugh. Once he started, he couldn't stop, the ridiculous idea of Jacob as a cartoon donkey settling into his head. Then he snorted, and that set Jacob off, his high-pitched laugh something that Trent always found hilarious, laughter feeding laughter until the car rang with their happiness.

Wheezing, holding his sides, he semi-yelled at Jacob, "Stop it. You're killing me."

"Oh, babe. That was classic." Jacob used thumb and finger of one hand to wipe his eyes, still laughing. "Classic."

"Har, har." A sign in front of a house down one of the side streets caught his attention, and he whipped around, staring at the building. "Jacob, turn around."

"What?" The car's speed didn't vary, and the trajectory was still straight ahead.

"Turn around. I want to go back and look at that house." Trent peered left and right, finally seeing a street sign just ahead. "Turn in there, and we'll go back."

"What about the grocery store?" The steady click said Jacob had listened, and a moment later, they had pulled into someone's driveway, leaving it just as quickly when Jacob reversed, deftly aiming the vehicle back the direction they'd come from. "Where was it?"

"Just there." He pointed at the road and peered up towards where he'd seen the For Sale sign. "See it?"

"Yeah." Jacob drove to the house slowly, his attention out the window much like Trent's was. "It's big, Trentie. Probably four bedrooms."

"Look at it, though. I didn't think we'd see anything like that here."

Two soaring stories in a neighborhood of flat ranch homes. The first floor had a wraparound porch, and the second had three distinct balconies that Trent could see. The two-car garage was off to the side, but attached, with what might be an apartment over the vehicle bays. White with slate blue trim. From the outside, there wasn't a single thing Trent would change.

"Hello, yes." Trent turned to see Jacob had his phone to his ear, squinting at the real estate agency's sign. "Is this Emily Delmonico?" A pause, then Jacob smiled, a sure sign he liked the response from whoever he was on the phone with. "Yes, I'm calling about a property you're representing on Echo Valley Road in Germantown." Another pause, and a thumbs-up gesture when Trent motioned impatiently. "Emily, can I put you on speaker? My husband is here in the car with me, and… Oh, that'd be lovely, five minutes? We're actually parked in front of the house now. Yes, sounds good. See you in a few." Jacob disconnected and stared at Trent, lips quirked in a tiny grin. "She's just two streets over, finishing an inspection. She can be here in five minutes. Wanna do a tour?"

"Let me think on it a minute. Ohmygodyes." Trent squeezed his eyes closed tightly. "It's going to have termites or mold, or I'll hate the floor plan."

"There's going to be leaks in the bathroom and the wiring will need to be replaced." Jacob helpfully picked up where Trent had left off. They went back and forth, listing all the things each of them could think of that would make them hate the house. He started the car again and eased into the driveway. "I don't know. I can't think of anything else."

"Let's get out and walk around the outside. Maybe we can rule it out based on property lines or something." Trent grabbed the door handle, then glanced back at Jacob. "But Jakey, what if?"

"We'll know in a few minutes if it's a flat no, a maybe, or a hell yes. Live in the ambiguity of not knowing for a change." Jacob was already out of the car by the time Trent had climbed out. "That's a big yard. A lot of grass to mow. Jericho would get a workout."

"I don't do ambiguity, Jakey."

"I know." Jacob walked towards the house, angling around the side. "There's another balcony over here."

"But what if we like it?" Trent's feet were stuck in place, cemented by uncertainty as tightly as if he were shackled.

"If we like it and we can afford it, we buy it." Jacob's voice floated from around the corner of the house as he disappeared to the back. "Oh, flower gardens. Those are pretty."

"Jakey." A car turned off the main street headed their way, signage plastered along the side matching what was in front of the house. "Jakey, she's here."

An hour and a half later, Trent and Jacob were back where they'd started, sitting in the car and looking up at the house. Trent absently lifted a hand as the agent tooted her horn, driving away. Now that he knew what was on the other side of the walls, he filled in the gaps with the memory of the dining room and kitchen, all of which was open to the family room spanning the back of the house. Big windows in every room, sunlight and fresh air available at a flick of the finger. Two-and-a-half-car garage, with plenty of room for a workbench and bike racks. And best of all, there was a downstairs room tucked along the side of the house that had already been divided for offices. The arrangement would give him and Jacob independent workspaces but have them only steps apart.

"That small bedroom upstairs would be perfect." Jacob was musing, his voice soft and low.

"Perfect for what? It's too small for Jericho." Trent laid his head back against the seat. "I thought the one at the other end of the hall from the master would be good for him."

"Yeah, that'd be the one for him. A little bit of privacy, but easy access to the kitchen. All the things a growing boy might need."

Jacob was still staring at the house as if he couldn't believe they'd found something like this when they weren't even looking. Not yet. The plan had been to come to Memphis and see Jaime, celebrate Jericho's birthday with family and friends, then go back home until the Christmas break. Jericho was set to start school in California in three weeks.

"We can't do this. There's not enough time." His subconscious threw him an image of the gorgeous subway tile backsplash over a farm sink just like one he'd been drooling over in a catalog. "It's a nice house, though. What'd you say about that little bedroom?"

"It'd be perfect." The sound of Jacob's sigh was heavy, filled with something...anticipation, maybe?

Trent turned to look at him. "Perfect for what, Jakey?"

Jacob started the car, throwing his arm over the seat back as he reversed out of the driveway. He paused, stared up at the house again, then faced forwards as he pulled away. When it came, his answer was soft, almost inaudible. The words still shook Trent to his core, making his nerves jangle.

"A nursery."

Chapter Eleven
Jericho

"I got this, Uncle Trent." Jericho paused on his way up the stairs, shifting the box in his arms until he could see around it. "This is the last one for my bedroom. I'm just going to unpack and get set up, and then I'll be back down to help in the kitchen." Trent's face was a mass of worry and exhaustion, an expression he'd worn for nearly the entire time he and Jake had been pursuing the real estate deal. *Man needs to chill out.* "Leave some boxes for me."

Trent flipped a hand at him that could have meant he was the most brilliant strategist ever at unpacking or indicated he was annoying as a gnat.

Jericho grinned.

Definitely a gnat.

Continuing on his way, he glanced in the other rooms on the second floor, able to do that because all the doors were wide open to facilitate the transport of boxes, just as he was doing right now. He'd only seen the house through pictures and one video walkthrough the agent had sent them after the paperwork was done and the painting Trent asked for had been completed. They hadn't bought the house, not yet. There just hadn't been time. The owners had worked out a lease deal for two months that allowed them to make the move from California in time for school to begin. Jake had already done most of whatever was needed for the actual purchase, and they expected that to go through before Halloween.

Then they'd well and truly be home. Something Jericho had never really experienced. He and his mom had moved every couple of years at a minimum. The farm had been the place they'd settled into longest, living there for nearly three years. But he'd known the houses were rentals, accustomed to brusque landlords making surprise inspections especially when the rent was late. The realization hadn't really hit him in California, maybe because his uncles were already settled into their house there, but the idea of living in a house that was *owned*, one that couldn't be taken away on a whim—he still couldn't get over the fact his bedroom had been painted just to suit him.

Rounding the doorframe, he stood for a moment, staring. His bedroom suite from California took up a chunk of the space but still left enough room for a desk and chair, something Jake had made a priority yesterday. They'd gone to a local furniture store, and when Jericho had paused at one set, a desk with a bookshelf, Jake had called a salesperson over immediately. Jericho looked around again. The walls were a soft sand color and the drapes were a rich sage. The effect felt entirely comfortable, soothing and safe, and his.

Shaking off the amazement, he set to work and within a short time was headed back downstairs. Trent was in the kitchen, a sea of opened boxes around him, none of them more than a quarter unpacked. He looked up and cried, "There you are," as if Jericho had been gone half his life.

It was moments like that when Jericho realized how desperately lucky he'd been that he had Trent and Jake. Forget the house or the things—it was the people in his life that made a difference, and as much as he'd loved his mother, he was still angry at her for withholding these treasures for such a long time. As he always did, he shoved those thoughts aside and waded in, looking for ways to help lift whatever burdens he could off his uncles. Not in any attempt to pay them back; he'd come to the realization a long time ago that how he'd been raised to think didn't factor with family. Now he just wanted to help so he could see more of the happy Trent, the joking Jake, and be surrounded by unstressed love from his little family.

"Put me to work." He swung in a half circle, glancing at the contents of all the boxes. "Where do you want me to start?"

"You're such a good boy." Trent pointed to a box near Jericho's feet. "That's pantry stuff."

He lifted and carried the box to the pantry, and within minutes had organized the contents on the shelves. He knew Trent would reorganize it, probably today, but at least it was out of the box and available. Jericho moved from box to box in that fashion, taking direction from Trent when offered, but all the boxes had to be unpacked eventually, so he knew he couldn't go wrong as long as he was helping.

His phone buzzed in his pocket a couple of times, but he ignored the device in favor of finishing faster. The caller would be Nate or Jordan, and the one could wait, while the other would be best answered in private anyway. He felt his cheeks heat up and bent double, hiding his face behind the flaps of a box.

The kiss.

The whirlwind trip around his birthday hadn't given them a chance to be alone again, not anywhere Jericho would have been comfortable for a repeat. But that didn't mean the whole experience didn't play on a loop in his head.

Staring at Jordan across the dining room table later that night, he hadn't been able to pull his gaze from the man's mouth. He'd felt off-balance, but in a good way. In an I-know-what-he-tastes-like way.

Then it had been time to return to California. Jordan had come over early the morning of their flight out, but Jericho had already been downstairs, helping Jaime in the kitchen. He'd been so tongue-tied and shy even Jaime had noticed, directing Jordan to assist with whatever he'd been working on. Jordan had bumped his shoulder, brushed the backs of his fingers with a touch, and at one point had pretended to swipe flour off Jericho's cheek—when neither of them had been near where Jaime was making biscuits.

Thank God that all the things Jericho saw as embarrassing, Jordan thought were cute.

Jericho rolled his eyes and finished with a box, efficiently breaking it down afterwards and stacking the cardboard with the rest. "Done." He looked around the kitchen with pride. "Done, done, and done. What do you want to start on next?"

"Dinner." Trent chuckled as he leaned an elbow on the kitchen island. "Then you need to get to bed early tonight. School tomorrow."

"Don't remind me." Jericho groaned. They'd arrived in the trucks two days ago and had been frantically unloading for most of yesterday so Jake could turn in the rentals. The unpacking wasn't finished and wouldn't be for a while, but this was his last day to really help because somehow in between everything else he had to do, Trent had managed to get all the paperwork he'd originally wrangled to California back to Tennessee. Jericho hadn't seen the school except from a distance as he'd ridden with Jake yesterday. Even from blocks away the building looked huge, and intimidating, especially when compared to the school he'd attended before. "I could take another week. They don't go over anything important for the first few days anyway."

"Nope. Tomorrow your butt is at a desk and you're back in learning mode." Trent offered him a semi-regretful smile. "Sorry, Charlie."

"That's okay. It's a sacrifice I'm willing to make." Jericho shook his head sadly, camping it up for his uncle.

"Oh, did I tell you the news?" Trent had turned away and was half inside the pantry, doing exactly what Jericho had expected, shuffling boxed and canned goods around. "Connor got that new job. He's going to be coaching at your school."

"Oh, yeah?" *Would it be weird having family around all the time?* He didn't know about that, but Connor was pretty cool, and it didn't hurt that Jordan thought highly of him. "That's awesome."

"Trent?" Jake's voice echoed in hard edges off unfamiliar surfaces within the house. Jericho couldn't pick out where the call had come from. "Where are you?"

"Kitchen." Trent twisted back and forth, looking around the rooms visible from where he stood, apparently also unable to decide where Jake was. "Where are you?"

"Offices." Jericho turned just in time to see Jake come into view, a wide smile on his face. "It's like a wild game of hide and seek, only you aren't really hiding."

"I could hide if you wanted, big boy." Trent's campy flirting made Jericho laugh.

"And on that note, I'm going to go to my room." He grabbed the new backpack Jake had shown up with earlier today, filled with bags from the local big box store. "Take a minute to organize my backpack." Trent opened his mouth, and Jericho shook his head. "Nu-uh. I never know where you've put things when you organize something. Plus, it'll give you guys time to do whatever it is Uncle Jake has on his mind." He took the stairs two at a time, calling over his shoulder. "I'm shutting my door. I don't want to hear anything."

Laughter followed him to his bedroom, and he did what he'd told them he would. Door closed, he set the bag on the floor, dropping down beside it. Before he started unpacking bags and opening packaging, he pulled out the phone. There were two missed video calls from Jordan, followed by a text that simply said, **Call me when you can**.

Propping the phone against a pillow on the bed, he initiated a video call, keeping his gaze on the screen as it connected and Jordan's blue eyes filled his view. "Hey, how's the apartment? Everything okay?"

Jordan'd had to return to campus early—all athletes were required to attend conditioning camp. It didn't matter that his scholarship sport didn't start for months; by the time Jericho had gotten back to Memphis, Jordan had already been gone. His third year was beginning, and Jordan had decided to leave the dorms behind, finding both an apartment and roommate through the college's housing department.

"Yeah, it's good. How's the move coming?" Jordan shifted the phone, and Jericho saw he was at what looked like a dining room table. From where he'd propped the phone, Jericho could see a couple of thick books opened, visible sections of text highlighted in yellow. "Is that your room?"

He smiled and nodded, glancing away from the phone to look around himself. "Yeah. It's awesome. I can't believe Trent was able to get it painted and everything before we moved in. We're close to unpacked now, finally."

"Enjoy it while you can." Jordan gestured to the walls behind where he sat. "Housing here is limited to about five colors. So far I think I've seen off-white, eggshell, white, ivory, and snow. It's a giddy moment to find something as off the hook as cream." Jericho laughed and Jordan smiled, one dimple creasing his cheek. "It looks good." He paused, and his cheeks reddened when he continued. "You look good."

"So do you." Jericho wished with everything inside him that Jordan wasn't a couple hundred miles away. Even though they were closer now, and he was certain to see Jordan at the holidays if not before, it still felt entirely too far.

"Jericho, I—" Jordan jerked out of frame as a pair of arms circled his shoulders, a stranger's face coming into view instead. Topped with a shock of dark hair, the deep brown eyes bored into Jericho.

"And who's this, lumpikins?" Lilting and bright, the man's voice expressed a great interest in the answer to his question.

"Daniel, get off me." Jordan reappeared, turned sideways so his face and Daniel's were close together. *Kissing distance*, Jericho thought. Jordan gripped the man's wrists and ripped them from around his neck. "Knock it off."

"But who's on the video, lover?" The casual way that word flowed from those reddened lips pierced Jericho's chest, spearing deep and making him jerk in pain. Jordan was still trying to pull free from the man's grip, but every time he'd remove one hand, the other would latch on somewhere else like an octopus. "Hmmm? Cheating on me already?"

Jericho's hand snapped out and his finger was only millimeters from the button that would disconnect the call when Jordan answered, his growled response enough to freeze Jericho in place. "It's my goddamned boyfriend, Daniel. Get the fuck off me."

Boyfriend.

"Well, why didn't you say so. This is the vaunted Jericho, then? Hi, sweetkins. Your lovely man here has done nothing but talk about you." The man pursed his lips, blowing a kiss at the camera. "Nothing but good things, of course. Hey…" His face came closer, eclipsing Jordan's. "You didn't think this was… Oh, honey. I'm sorry. I was just messing with him. Trust me, Jordan's not interested in any booty but yours. Promise."

Jericho opened his mouth, but nothing came out. Daniel frowned, staring at him. "Serious, Jericho, he's all about you. I was just playing around. Jordan, I think something's wrong."

The view on the screen shifted, and then Jordan's face filled the screen, his blue eyes looking worried now. "Jericho, that's Daniel, my roommate."

"Boyfriend." His voice didn't lift on the end, so he wasn't questioning Jordan, but still, the word slipped free.

Jordan frowned, his head tipped to the side, and a lock of hair fell across his brow. "Yeah, Jericho. Boyfriend. You're my boyfriend. Daniel, the *ass*hole, is my roommate."

"Boyfriend."

Daniel's voice came from somewhere in the distance; he must have moved away to grant some privacy. Still, he was close enough to hear their exchange, because he told Jordan, "He's cute. I like him."

Jordan's head snapped sideways, brows drawing down in a dark scowl that didn't do anything to mask his handsome features. Jericho watched the lines of his jaw tighten and clench. *So hot.* "He's mine, Daniel. Keep your eyes to yourself."

"I'm your boyfriend." Jericho huffed out a light laugh. "I have a boyfriend. You're my boyfriend."

Jordan's eyes were dancing when he looked back at the camera. "Yeah, didn't you get that when we were at the coffee shop?"

The last day of the initial trip to Memphis, Jordan had taken Jericho to a mall. The plan had been to see a movie and grab a bite to eat, but the place had been filled with distractions, and by the time they'd made it to the theater, the movie had already started. So they'd simply walked the mall, circling first the downstairs and then the upper floor. Along the way, they'd stopped in a tiny shop specializing in varied coffee drinks. As they'd stood in line, Jordan's hand had found his and latched on, clasping so tightly Jericho couldn't have pulled away if he'd wanted. Jericho had glanced around but never caught anyone looking at them at all. As if the connection, small as it was, had been a normal occurrence here.

They'd gone through to the register like that, paired, and when they had to separate to take their drinks, Jordan had steered them to a tiny table near the back wall, scooting his chair around so he sat next to Jericho, the outside of their thighs pressed tight together. Jordan had leaned in as they talked, his arm propped along the back of Jericho's chair, the position a blatant intimacy orchestrated by Jordan and something Jericho had loved. When they'd finally left the shop, Jordan's hand had again found his, and they'd finished walking through the mall like that, hand in hand.

"No. I mean. I kinda." Jericho shook his head, the tingling in his belly a distraction. The butterflies were out in force today. It was like this every time he and Jordan spoke, but talking to Jordan at the same time he was remembering how it had felt to have the world blocked out, be protected by him? He was on anticipation overload. "I mean I hoped."

"Well, stop hoping, and just know. *God*." Jordan thrust a hand through his hair, looking frustrated. "I wish I was there." The background shifted as light sources changed, and a door closing told him Jordan had taken the phone into his bedroom. "I wish I was there and could do more than just look at you."

Jericho reached for his phone as he climbed on the bed and curled up on his side. He held the screen right in front of his face, feeling the same way he had when Jordan had kissed him. "I wish you were here, too."

Cherished.

Trent

Lifting his head, Trent stared around the office, unsure what had pulled his attention away from the work on his screen. No noise in the house; Trent was the only one home right now, Jacob having stepped out to pick a few things up at the store. Trent angled his head as if that would help him listen more intently, then stood, rolling his chair back. He was on edge for some reason, the silence now seeming sinister.

"Jakey?" Just in case Jacob had returned home and Trent hadn't heard him, he called out, "Honeybuns, you here?"

Silence met his inquiries, and he crazily wished for a dog in that instant. A dog would be company and would be a good alert system if someone did break in. *Not that I think anyone's breaking in.* His heart was thudding along quickly, faster than before, the errant thought of a stranger crawling through a broken window enough to make his palms sweat.

"Jakey?" He paused at the bottom of the stairs, looking up only to be met by stillness and quiet. Turning, he surveyed the main floor and was pleased to find zero intruders. Walking into the kitchen, he was pulling a glass down from the shelf when something buzzed behind him. Juggling the glass for a couple of twisty tumbles, he clutched it against his chest as he turned, breathing heavily.

Jacob's phone was on the charging pad, and as he glared at it the device vibrated again, the racket reverberating through the wood. That had to have been what he'd heard or sensed. "Oh my God."

Glass filled with cold orange juice, he set the drink on the counter and picked up Jacob's phone, using his thumbprint to unlock the screen. There was a flood of text messages in view, from four or five people, and he exited that display, navigating directly to the text message software. Connor, Jaime, Jericho, and Jordan had all messaged Jacob in the past fifteen minutes. Trent checked the clock and clucked softly. Jericho was in class and shouldn't be texting, so he made a mental note to have a conversation with him tonight. It wasn't often Jericho did anything out of line; he was the ultimate good kid. Trent wanted to attribute that to Stella more than himself and Jacob, but he knew from the bits and pieces Jericho had dropped over the past months that Stella had had little to do with molding the boy into the man he would one day be.

Another text came in, this from Connor. Trent picked up his juice and took a drink as he touched the text, expanding the full contents. A second later juice had sprayed out his nose and mouth, covering the countertop in front of him.

Did you miss the fact the baby's coming? James asked when you'll be here. She wants you to bring bacon.

It was accompanied by a picture of Jaime in a hospital bed, giving the bowl of green Jell-O in front of her a scowling thumbs-down.

Jericho texted next, and Trent wisely didn't have a mouthful of anything when he read it.

I got a ride. Jordan's coming home for the baby. Tell Aunt Jaime good luck.

Through the door to the garage, the sound of a motor swelled then cut off, and Trent was staring in anticipation at the doorway when it opened. Jacob backed through it, his arms full of grocery bags. He turned and spied Trent, a sweet smile tugging at his lips.

"Taking a breather?" Jacob plunked the bags on the island and walked around to prop his hands on either side of Trent's hips. "Missed you." Trent dipped his chin for a kiss, eyes closed as Jacob repeated the caress, the tip of his tongue trailing across Trent's lips. "What's up?"

"Jaime's having the baby."

Jacob stopped moving. If it weren't for his pupils dilating wide, Trent could have wondered if the man had been flash-frozen in place.

"You forgot your phone." He held it up, wiggling it back and forth in front of Jacob's face. "They've been blowing it up. You've got texts from everyone." Jacob still hadn't moved, was scarcely breathing. "Wanna get ready to go to the hospital?" Jacob blinked slowly, pupils narrowing to tiny dots. "Honeybuns? James wants her brudder. Let's go see this baby born."

Another slow blink, then Jacob pushed close, his mouth demandingly tight against Trent's. Eyes wide open, they kissed, a hard press of lips that conveyed every ounce of Jacob's excitement and anticipation.

"My sister's having a baby." Jacob breathed the words, lips moving against Trent's as he spoke. "James is gonna be a momma again."

"She is." Gripping Jacob's shoulders, Trent moved him back a couple of steps. "You need to do anything here before we go?" He angled a look at the grocery bags on the island. "Groceries?"

"I got it," Jacob said, whirling and moving to unpack things. "Get your shoes on. By the time you're ready, I'll have the cold stuff put away. Go." He glanced over his shoulder at Trent, who hadn't moved. "Go already. James is having a baby."

"So I heard." Jacob's phone vibrated in Trent's grip and he glanced down, laughing at the message. "She wants bacon and a margarita, both of which I think would be forbidden in the birthing suite."

"*Go*." Jacob turned back to the groceries, and Trent did as he was told.

"James, she's so flippin' gorgeous I can't even *breathe* when I look at her. Princess, you're the most beautiful thing I've ever seen. You're gonna be a heartbreaker, I just know it. Gonna keep Daddy awake at night guarding the door."

Trent glanced up at Jaime's laughter, then immediately turned his focus back on the baby girl in his arms. "Momma thinks your Uncle Trentie's funny, baby girl. But he's right. She's gonna find out in fifteen years or so. Uncle Trentie's right. Yes, he is. That's right."

"Gimme." There was a cautious nudge at his shoulder, and Trent cut his eyes over to see Jacob standing there, arms outstretched, impatiently waiting. "My turn. Stop being such a baby hog."

Trent smiled at him, then carefully transferred the precious cargo from his arms to Jacob's. He stared, transfixed, as Jacob curled in around the baby girl, head bent to gaze into his niece's face. That lock of hair fell across his brow, the corners of his eyes crinkled, and the softest, sweetest smile Trent had ever seen curled the corners of Jacob's lips.

"Caitlynn, sweetheart." Voice a barely there croon, Jacob slowly bounced the baby in his arms, swaying from foot to foot. "Look at you. Just look at you."

My husband needs a baby.

He'd known Jacob wanted kids, plural, for a long time. Since well before Jaime'd had Matt, now a three-year-old terror. But seeing Jacob like this, holding a newborn, Trent made a silent but determined vow that he'd make this happen for them. Not just for Jacob, because Trent would love to have a child, too, but mostly because of the expression of devotion and adoration on Jacob's face right now. All that love needed to go somewhere, and a baby was the perfect target.

"Do you see that?" Jaime's throaty question was voiced from behind him, and Trent unwillingly pulled his gaze away from Jacob and the baby to look at his sister-in-law. She blinked back tears, her words vibrating with emotion when she told him something he'd already decided. "He needs one of those, Trentie." The love on Jaime's face was so much like what always shone through Jacob, and Trent realized that as much as he wanted it for Jacob, Jaime did also.

"You could make it easy on me and just give us this one?" He bent and brushed a kiss across her cheek, hearing her laughter up close. "Seriously, you make pretty babies, Jaime. Caitlynn is perfect."

"Mine." The granite strength of the single word came from Connor standing on the other side of the bed. "You can't have her."

He looked between the two of them and decided to share the good news that had been somewhat sidelined since the move. "We were picked by a surrogate." At Jaime's pleased inrush of breath, he held up a cautioning hand. "Because of the house and everything happening so fast, we asked for a six-month furlough. She might not wait through the deferment, and we wouldn't blame her. She said she understood why, with the move, and we assured her it wasn't for lack of wanting or being a hundred percent onboard with a baby. If she's selected another couple, it's back to the drawing board, either in California or here."

"I'd do it in a heartbeat." With her chin lifted like that, Jaime looked so much like her stubborn brother that Trent had to lean in and kiss her cheek again. "Whatever y'all need."

"I love you, you know that?" A palm landed in the middle of his back, heat blossoming from the touch, and Trent turned to see Jacob standing behind him, passing tiny Caitlynn to her father. "James, just knowing you'd go through that for us is an honor. I love you, too."

Trent leaned against Jacob. He didn't have to question if his husband would hold him up or would support him through thick and thin. He knew. Just like he knew Jacob would be there for any child they had. None of the questions that terrified Trent even pinged Jacob's radar.

"I married an all-in kinda guy." He turned his face and ducked, burying his nose against Jacob's neck, breathing in his scent.

"Hate to break it to you, but that's not news." Jacob's quiet laughter rumbled through them both, the vibrations transferring through to Trent. "I think it's time for us to vamoose." Trent looked up to see Jaime shifting sideways in the bed, pillow strategically placed at her side as Connor hovered close by, Caitlynn cradled against his chest.

"Little momma, we're going to head out." Jaime nodded, but she had eyes only for her daughter, and Trent smiled at the sight. *Perfection*. "Love you, sweet girl."

Fingers twined together, they rode the elevator down, exited at the lobby. Just outside the door, Trent stumbled as Jacob slowed, tugging at his hand. He turned to see Jacob's attention fixed across the parking lot. Squinting, he saw Jordan climb out of his car but choked when Jacob's hand covered his mouth just as he was about to shout a welcome. Focused intensely, he watched Jordan trot around the front of the vehicle to open the passenger door. A moment later, Jericho appeared, wedged between Jordan and the side of the car. Jordan herded him sideways, closed the door, then leaned in close.

Trent whirled, fisting the fabric of Jacob's shirt as he buried his face against his throat. "I can't see this."

"Babe." Soft wonder suffused Jacob's voice, and Trent twisted far enough to glance over his shoulder. He was just in time to see the two boys break apart, neither going too far from the other. "That's sweet devotion. Did you see how Jordan opened the car door for Jericho? Oh, man. He's got it bad."

"That's my nephew." Trent knew his argument didn't hold any conviction and was unsurprised when Jacob just laughed at him. "I can't see that. It's against the dad-slash-uncle code. If I see it, I think the rules say I have to beat up Jordan. Or at least give him a stern talking-to. That's Jericho, he's my baby."

Jacob arched away from Trent and stared up at him, eyebrows raised.

Before Jacob could say it, Trent filled in the silence with an entirely sarcastic "Babe" that had his husband shouting with laughter as Trent grumbled.

"I wasn't being funny."

Chapter Twelve
Jericho

"So, that was weird."

Jericho leaned his head against the passenger seat in Jordan's car. They were just leaving the hospital after the strangest visit he could have ever conceived.

He and Jordan had scarcely been out of the car when they heard Jake, and looking up they saw both of his uncles standing in the hospital parking lot. Then, even though they'd clearly been leaving, both Trent and Jake had accompanied him and Jordan up to Jaime's room. They'd knocked and been called inside, only to find Jaime in the process of nursing Caitlynn. Jericho hadn't known where to direct his eyes, so he'd finally settled on staring Coach Connor in the face.

"I'm so awkward around stuff like that." He was staring out the window and realized they hadn't moved. He looked at Jordan to find him smiling, one of the deadly dimples on full display. "What?"

"You were very sweet."

Jordan stretched out a hand and Jericho clasped it, watching as their fingers threaded together. It was the most natural thing, an action that had happened dozens of times now, but he was just as floored by the ease and comfort now as he had been the first time.

"I was weird. Did you hear how loud I was?" He'd spent the first ten minutes aggressively engaging Coach about school, dissecting his schedule and how it lined up with the one Coach had to follow. "I'm surprised they didn't throw me out."

"They didn't mind." Jordan leaned closer, one hand lifting to cup the side of Jericho's neck.

The air in the car had thinned to that of the atmosphere on the moon. That was the only explanation for how hard it was for Jericho to take a full breath in. He wheezed out, "That baby, though. She's adorable."

"So precious. She looks just like Matt did when he was born." Jordan angled Jericho's jaw just enough to trail a wet line of kisses up, ending at the sensitive skin behind his ear. "Jericho." His name was scarcely a whisper, an indrawn rush of air formed around the consonants that represented him. "You know what you do to me?"

"I hope I make you crazy." Heart jumping in his chest, he could hear the pounding of each beat of blood through his veins as a tom-tom in his ears. His words were far bolder than he felt, butterflies filling his throat until he shivered under Jordan's hands. "Because that's what you do to me."

Jordan leaned close and rested his head on Jericho's shoulder. He lifted their clasped fingers to his mouth and pressed a hard kiss against Jericho's knuckles. The unsteady rhythm of his breaths testified he was just as affected as Jericho, which was comforting for some reason.

They'd talked at some length about how far they were willing to go right now. With the separation and distance between them, the reasonable timeframes and suggestions all made sense. Right now, with Jordan's weight pinning him into the seat, Jericho was ready to throw it all out the window. He'd make up a new plan right here on the spot that included going back to somewhere that had a horizontal surface and setting up camp there.

"Your dads invited me for supper."

Jericho startled and pulled away, staring at Jordan in confusion. "My dads?"

"Your uncles." Jordan moved back behind the steering wheel, and Jericho missed the closeness immediately, wishing he hadn't initiated any kind of retreat. "I forget sometimes they aren't, you know? They act like dads, and that's how you treat them."

"My dad died before I knew him." Jericho had two pictures of himself as an infant with a man his mom had labeled his father. "My stepdad, well, you know what he did." Jordan did, too. He knew all of it, more than Jericho had ever told anyone else, spending hours upon hours purging himself of the ugliness Frank had left behind. The shame and terror he thought he'd gotten past, but when he woke from a nightmare, he was under standing orders to call Jordan, no matter the time. It was during those late-night video chat sessions that Jordan had taken control of the conversations, steering them so Jericho felt safe enough to talk about how much he'd feared Frank, how angry he was at his mom for putting them both in that situation. Jordan hadn't judged, hadn't said a single thing about blame for anyone—except Frank. It was like that first conversation Jericho had had with Jake, where he'd seen his uncle fight rage he'd felt on Jericho's behalf. "I guess they do act like dads."

"Trent threatened to buy me condoms." Jericho stared at Jordan in disbelief as his face grew uncomfortably hot. He ducked his chin, doing his best to avoid Jordan's gaze. "Hey, no, Jericho. Don't feel bad. It's no big deal." There was laughter in Jordan's voice when he said, "I just told him I had my own stash." Jericho tipped his head back, eyes closed as he struggled to take in a breath through the laughter threatening to burst out of him at the idea of Trent hearing those words. As open as his uncles were about their own relationship, Trent had been reluctant to even admit to what Jericho was building with Jordan. He'd stuffed his fingers in his ears one day rather than hear Jake gently teasing about Jericho's boyfriend. Jordan chuckled, amusement vibrating his voice as he continued talking. "I'm not sure what he thought I'd say, but it wasn't that. He sputtered for a good two minutes. It was so bad, Jacob had to rescue him."

"Oh, God. What did Daddy Jake do?" Jericho shivered and shook his head vigorously. "You know what? That sounds way too weird. I can't do it. Nope, can't do it. Take two: What'd Uncle Jake do?"

"No threats. He just said he expected our firstborn to be named after him."

Jericho slumped in the seat, scrunching down so his butt was hanging off into space, head far below the level of the window. "My family is so insane."

"No." Jordan had kept his grip on Jericho's hand and lifted the backs of his knuckles to his lips for another gentle kiss. "That's just how family is."

Jericho leaned against the fender of Jordan's car, feet spread wide enough for Jordan to stand between his legs. The house rose behind where they were parked in the driveway, the only light from inside visible through Jericho's bedroom window, the dim square shedding only slight illumination. The moon overhead cast a glow bright enough to see Jordan's face, and that was all Jericho needed. The cries of cicadas said that dusk was past, nighttime dimming the landscape, settling cool shadows around everything. Jericho's hands were on Jordan's waist, and as Jordan pressed a final brushing touch against his lips, he had to concentrate to not clench tightly, not try to hold him in place.

Another pass of Jordan's lips on his, and Jericho felt the heat and wet from a slow swipe of Jordan's tongue. Breathing fast, he opened his mouth in invitation. Jordan groaned and slanted his mouth across Jericho's, the silken glide of his tongue a confident caress Jericho never wanted to end.

Jordan broke free, burying his head in Jericho's neck with a growling groan. "God. I need to go."

"I know." They'd been saying the same things for half an hour, and Jericho knew he needed to be the one to call an end to it or Jordan would be driving late into the night to get back to school. "And I want you to be safe. Get there safely, and then at the end of the year, come back safe to me." He didn't know where this unaccustomed confidence was coming from, but he gave his mouth free rein, letting it run away with him. "Because from where I sit, Jordan, you're mine. I know I'm not very old, but I know how I feel. I've only got this year and two more, and I'll be in college or working."

"You're not too young to know your own mind." Jordan straightened, looking into Jericho's face, his expression intent. "You're not too young for me, period. Jericho, I'm willing to wait as long as you need me to. I'll wait for you. You're worth it, Jericho. So worth it. I'll wait for you." Jordan crowded closer as he spoke, their bodies pressed together as he dropped his head to claim another kiss Jericho willingly gave up.

Those words rang through Jericho's head, not just that night, but through the upcoming weeks and months.

"I'll wait for you."

Chapter Thirteen
Trent

"Jakey." Head resting on Jacob's shoulder, Trent stared at the screen of the computer, his eyes fixed on the shifting image. The speakers went silent for a moment, then hissed and spat, and he tensed all over as he heard the rapid doubled thudding sound again. Reverently, he whispered, "Those are our babies."

Jacob's arm tightened around his shoulders, fingers digging in hard enough Trent knew he'd be sporting bruises later. He didn't care.

Jaime squealed and rounded the desk, wrapping both of them in her arms. "So you went to the sonogram this morning? Do they know the sexes yet?" Jaime didn't give either of them a chance to answer, interrupting herself as she kept jabbering. "Babies move around so much, and with two of them, I bet it's harder yet. But just listen to those little ones. So strong. Jake, those are your babies. Those are yours and Trent's babies. Did you tell them that Auntie Jaime loves them? Because she does. So much." She was crying by the end, and Trent drew her in between himself and Jacob, bringing her into their embrace.

"They are." Jacob's voice held all the wonder he'd shown at the clinic earlier that day. "That sound is our little babies."

After the deferment period ended, they'd terminated the contract with the California clinic, opting instead to go through one in Memphis. After looking at the choices, they'd wound up selecting the same clinic that had brought Jaime and Connor together, liking the vibe they got from the case handler. Faster than Trent had anticipated, they'd been matched with an egg donor and surrogate and, after a getting-to-know-you period, had decided to move forwards with the process.

After two failed IVF attempts, they'd gotten lucky with a third, and their surrogate—a sweet single mother Jacob said reminded him of Jaime—was five months pregnant with twins. Jericho had just started his junior year of high school, Jordan was in his final year of college—and just after the first of the year, they'd be bringing home two newborns, moving them into that little bedroom that Jacob had been right about; it was just right for a nursery.

They'd gone with the swirl method, mixing their semen and letting the randomness of fate determine the biological makeup of the child...children. He had to keep reminding himself that they were going to have two babies.

It caught up to him at odd moments, and the fear was never far behind. But all he had to do was catch a glimpse of Jacob's face as he talked about their children and see the awe, the pure love his husband already had for the babies, and the fear would ebb away.

"She's twenty weeks." Trent gave Jaime a squeeze. "We've got one of each. A little girl and a little boy."

He winced at Jaime's shriek and looked over her shoulder at Jacob, who was making the same face. "Oh my God. That's perfect. That's absolutely perfect."

Trent stared at Jacob smiling wide, so much joy in his expression that Trent knew he'd never again question if they were doing the right thing.

"It absolutely is."

Chapter Fourteen

Epilogue

Jericho

He watched for the signal, and when the speaker patted the air with both palms, Jericho sat in a swish of polyester, the fabric bunching around his knees. The weight of the mortarboard on his head was unfamiliar, and he angled his neck only slightly to verify his random plucking at the gown was actually straightening the folds.

The next speaker droned on and on, and Jericho could feel himself losing focus. He blinked rapidly and straightened in the seat only to slump again immediately. If he'd had his way, he would have skipped the ceremony entirely, but as always, his uncles pulled the "we know better" card, and paired with Coach's prod of "these are good memories to have," Jericho had acquiesced. Hence his position right now on the inside aisle of a long row of chairs directly in front of the low stage built on the gymnasium floor.

To his direct left was Keith Carson, a boy he'd gotten to know fairly well over the years he'd been in the school, due to the alphabet and weekly assemblies. He glanced over to see Keith's eyes were glazed, and he looked much as Jericho felt. When his friend's head nodded sharply, he suppressed a snort of laughter, instead leaning close and calling his name. "Keith, don't fall over, yeah?" Keith's head shot up and he blinked, turning to look at Jericho. "You awake, man?"

"Yeah." The quiet response earned them a frown from the girl on Keith's other side, Darreylle Carmel. Jericho and Keith ignored her hissed shush, and Jericho rolled his eyes, causing Keith to chuckle. "Thanks."

Attention back on the stage, Jericho was surprised to see a different speaker had taken the place at the podium. He mentally consulted the program and realized that next would be the students, salutatorian and then valedictorian, and then the graduating seniors would walk the walk they'd been practicing for a week. And then—it'd be done.

And after years and months of waiting, he and Jordan would be together.

Chin up, he studied the line of adults in their own versions of the gowns the graduates wore. Attention reflectively directed to the speaker, they didn't fidget or wiggle. No foot tapping for these honored attendees. His uncle Jake sat up there alongside Coach. As Jericho stared at them, Jake cut a glance at Jericho, offering him a small smile and a nod before turning back to the speaker. He didn't know how Jake had pulled it off, but him being the one to hand Jericho his diploma mattered more than his uncle would ever know.

Uncle. He snorted. Jordan had hit it right so long ago when he'd likened their treatment of him to that of a father. Their relationships seemed to be ever-evolving, in good ways. These days, with the twins babbling about Papa and Dada, sometimes it was just easier to go with the flow. In the kitchen with Jake and the babies not two days ago, he'd called his uncle Papa and turned around to find Jake staring down into the sink with a stupidly wide smile on his face.

The babies had been a revelation. Something else he hadn't expected to like, and now he couldn't imagine life without them. Going away to school was going to kill him, and by the time they were barely a year old, he'd already dialed back his college selections from ones within a two- or three-hour radius of home to good old U of M right here in Memphis. Anything else was just too far. Jordan had already finished college and was lined up to start a paid position as a clerk at a law firm here. His plan was to earn money for a couple of years before he went to the next step of graduate school, with the goal of eventually sitting for his LSATs and the bar and becoming a lawyer. Something Jericho had learned about his boyfriend over the years was he made plans and stuck with them, working every detail until he got the most preferred outcome.

He knew if he looked over his shoulder, he'd see Trent wrangling little Charlotte and Jackson with help from Nate. He rolled his eyes. Trent hadn't realized they'd named their babies after southern towns until after it was too late to make changes. The first time he'd caught Jake rocking little Jack while humming the tune to Jackson, Trent had officially lost his shit. Jack and Lottie were both sweet kids, and Jericho had spent more nights than he'd want to admit in the nursery, just listening to them breathe.

Applause rose around him, and he brought his hands together without much effort, not a golf clap but just one that wouldn't even redden his palms.

The salutatorian's speech was five minutes, max, and during the returned applause, the speakers were again shuffling across the stage, changing places in a choreographed round of musical chairs.

"I don't have anything to tell you that you don't already know." Jericho looked up at the boy's matter-of-fact tone. White knuckles gripping the edges of the podium seemed to make that delivery a lie. "You already know there's no magic potion to make life easier. No wave of the wand that will smooth the way. Work, more work, and a little more work will take you much farther down the road than standing in the ditch and wishing upon a star. If you're willing to put in the work, then you reap the rewards."

Jericho's head dipped as he studied his hands. Just from looking at them, no one would ever know that one had been far weaker than the other for a long time. Careful exercise had fixed the deficit, but it hadn't been as easy as he would have liked. Talking to the counselor his uncles had insisted on, he'd made a comment about it being a metaphor for his life. The man didn't disagree. Jericho had joked once that he wished he could drop his arm off at the gym and pick it up when it was toned and conditioned, like a batch of dry cleaning. Trent had stopped him in his tracks with a casual, "Gotta earn it to appreciate it."

That, too, could be said about so much of his life, after he'd landed with his uncles.

They'd given their love and acceptance freely, but their respect he'd had to earn. He looked up at Jake again, surprised to find him staring down at Jericho, the expression on his face filled with a mixture of pride and sadness.

His dreams occasionally took him back to Knoxville. Back to the barn, to the hospital, to the house where Frank had left him for dead.

When he woke, sometimes it took a few moments to remember all that had happened from then to now. There'd been more than once he'd woken and gone to sit just outside Trent and Jake's room, just to be close to them, a reminder that this was his life now.

Jake had found him one night, nearly tripped on him as he drowsily headed to the kitchen for a drink in the middle of the night. He hadn't questioned anything, hadn't demanded any kind of explanation, just slid down the wall next to Jericho until he was seated on the floor, legs stretched out in front of him, ankles crossed. Then Jake had talked about work, and the house, and Nate. He'd discussed the divisiveness of the HOA when it came to strains of grass seed, and how the HOA hadn't been on his radar when they bought the house, or they might have picked a different place to live. Then Jericho heard the babies on the monitor, stirring and beginning that soft coo that meant they'd woken up sweetly. Jake had leaned over and bumped their shoulders together. "Come help me with the babies."

And he had.

They'd spent an hour with the babies. Feeding, then changing, then rocking to sleep.

Sometime later, Jericho had climbed out of bed, aiming for the kitchen and an early breakfast. He'd found Jake asleep in the hallway, back propped against Jericho's doorframe, legs stretched out across the opening, barring the entrance. Without asking, without knowing for sure, Jake had just wanted to ensure Jericho was okay.

And that, in a nutshell, summed up his uncles and his life with them.

The row of students beside Jericho stood, and he belatedly lurched to his feet, earning another scowl from Darreylle. He turned and followed Keith between the chairs, out alongside the bleachers, and in a slow, student-by-student advancement to the stage. He watched Keith take that final step up, saw him stride across the surface, and counted to ten like they'd been told.

On his second footfall up the steps, he saw Jake peer around the superintendent, his smile evident even in the tiny portion of his face Jericho could see. Hand out, Jericho greeted the administrator, then pivoted around him and found his uncle Jake there with his diploma. Jericho ignored his outstretched hand, shuffling close and wrapping his arms around Jake instead.

"You done good, son." That whisper was everything.

Jericho pulled back, tears smearing his vision until Jake was just a blur. Something was shoved in his hand, and a steady grip on his shoulders steered him the direction he needed to go. He swiped at his eyes, quickly striking the tears from his face, and remembered to turn and look out into the audience. Trent stood in a sea of people, a child on each hip, tears streaming down his cheeks. "I love you, Uncle Trent."

Jericho realized that shout had come from him when Trent smiled and shouted back, "I love you too, Jericho."

Then he was down the steps and set to walk the circumference of the gymnasium to get back to his assigned place in the student seating.

Jericho had nearly caught up with Keith when someone stepped out in front of him.

It only took a moment to realize who it was.

The double dimples were out in force, and Jericho was pretty sure they'd eventually be the death of him.

Jordan wrapped one arm around his waist, his other hand going to the side of Jericho's face, and he brought their lips together in a hard, closemouthed kiss. "Proud of you." Jordan's thumb passed across Jericho's bottom lip, one side to another and back again. "See you in a few minutes."

Jericho nodded and released his hold on Jordan's arms, letting him step backwards. Jordan gripped his hand for a moment, their fingers twining together like always. Arms stretched out between them, Jordan was ready to let go when Jericho changed his mind.

Hands clasped, fingers threaded together, Jericho walked up the aisle, persistently tugging at Jordan until he laughingly acquiesced, following along.

Jericho had already decided he wasn't ever going to let go.

Chapter Fifteen

Epilogue

Jake

Stretched out on the couch, he had just shoved a pillow under his head and relaxed when he heard noises on the baby monitor. He tensed, prepared to swing into action because Trent was taking a shower that would probably turn into a multi-chapter bath. That meant Jake was on baby duty, and he didn't mind one bit. The noises subsided, leaving just the crooning murmur of the music box still playing in their room.

It had been a busy day, and Trent had outdone himself both with the plans for the party and the amount of stress he'd put on himself to get everything perfect. Jake knew Jericho wouldn't have cared one way or the other—he took after Jake that way. Trent had fussed over the guest list and the timing of the party; since the entire graduating class threw parties over the course of the same weekend, he hadn't wanted Jericho's to overlap with too many other popular kids. Wanted Jericho to have the best possible experience.

Jericho had come to Jake not even a week ago, concerned about Trent's insistence on every detail.

"You just gotta let him run with it." He looked up from washing the sink full of bottles and sippy cups that still seemed to accumulate multiple times a day. No matter how old the twins were, there was no getting around the fact that it took two of everything to keep their household going these days. He grinned down at the water. Not that he'd want it any other way. "I'll tell you a secret about your uncle, but you can't say anything to him. It's something he probably doesn't even know about himself." He stacked another batch of cups in the rinse sink, moving the next cache into the soapy water.

Jericho bumped his hip, and Jake took a half step to the side, making room for his self-appointed helper. Jericho had been like this since they'd been gifted him, always finding ways to ease the way. For a long time, they'd worried he was trying to compensate for not being able to save his mother, but the counselor put those worries to rest. Jericho was just a genuinely good guy, with a larger-than-normal reservoir of helpfulness.

"Okay. What's the secret?" Jericho turned on the hot water, rinsing each item and placing it in the dish drainer.

"His parents kicked him out of the house three months before his high school graduation. He got his diploma, but he did it by sleeping on couches and in his car, eating the free rolls at the cafeteria, and studying in the county library where the librarian took it upon herself to feed him. He did it working at the local grocery store, pumping gas at the gas station, and mowing yards. He did it by the skin of his teeth, but he did it." Jake placed another mess of cups and lids into the sink next to Jericho's hands, not surprised that the boy was watching him and not the work to be done. "He borrowed a gown to walk across the stage, and not one person cheered for him."

"Because he's gay." The painful finality in Jericho's voice tore at Jake, making him flinch. "I remember them, you know? They never seemed like bad people. Just very strict. Stuck in the past. Mom was different around them. When I think back on holidays and stuff, she was...smaller, I think."

"Yeah. He was outed, not of his choosing. Walked into their living room in the middle of a war. His father threatened to kill him, and to this day, Trent is convinced if he hadn't run with just the clothes on his back, he'd be dead now."

Jericho's soft, "Oh my God," and collapse to his elbows on the countertop weren't unexpected. He was Trent's nephew after all. Jake wanted to reach for him, to support him, but he knew leaving Jericho to fight through this on his own would make it a lesson he could call back on as he matured. The instant his uncle took on larger-than-life properties by surviving such a harsh situation.

"Your uncle Trent didn't get to have a graduation party. I think he sees this as his way to make sure you don't ever suffer the same deprivations." Jake tumbled the last of the lids and tiny plastic cutlery into Jericho's sink, pulling the plug on his to let the water drain. *"So we're going to let him do whatever it takes to make this party what he needs. He's going to make himself crazy, and in the process make us crazy, but it's what he wants to do, and that's good enough for me."*

"Me too." Jericho sucked in a long breath, his shoulders expanding with the inrush of air. He straightened and looked down at Jake, having topped him in height a year ago. *"I love him."* The hot water turned on and Jericho stared at the sink for a moment, then began methodically rinsing each item. *"Love you too, Uncle Jake."*

Arm thrown around Jericho's shoulders, Jake tugged him sideways into a hug. "And I love you too, son."

The door from the garage opened, and Jake sat up to look over, seeing Jericho and Jordan walking in. "Hey, boys." He'd learned to announce his presence early, loudly, and often when it came to those two. Jericho was eighteen now, and Jake had taken care of "the talk" long ago, even understanding that the boys had decided to wait until Jericho was out of high school to take anything to the next step. He knew from experience how impatient passion could be, and while he didn't really want to know if they'd stuck to it, he hoped for Jericho's sake they had. Eighteen and twenty-one seemed less of an age gap than sixteen and nineteen, and it had been a joy watching both boys mature over the years.

Jordan might dote on Jericho, but his nephew never took it for granted, which spoke to his personality. Jordan, for his part, still looked at Jericho like he hung the moon. It didn't mean they didn't argue, because Jake had been privy to the aftereffects of a couple of those. Jericho on a rant could nearly equal Trent, even if Jake would never tell his lover that fact.

"Hey, Uncle Jake." Jericho leaned against Jordan, hands clasped tightly. "Is Uncle Trent in bed already?"

"Bath." Jake shot him a grin, then subsided back on his pillow. "Twins are sleeping."

"Okay." Listening closely, he'd expected to hear footsteps heading towards the stairs and Jericho's room, but he saw them walking around the end of the couch instead. The boys settled on the other couch, Jordan wedged into the corner and Jericho leaned into his side. "Whacha watchin'?"

"No idea." He rolled his neck, looking at Jericho over the arm of the couch he was on. "Whacha doin'?" Not that the boys didn't watch TV with him or Trent, but this time of night it wasn't their normal routine. Plucking at the thread of nervousness he saw in Jericho's face, he swung his legs to the floor and sat up facing them. "Need to talk?"

"Maybe?"

Might as well defuse the tension with humor, he thought. "Jordan, did you knock my nephew up?"

Jordan grinned at him, shaking his head. "No, sir. But—" He bumped Jericho with an elbow. "Someone has something they want to ask about."

"Jordie." Jericho's head twisted around, and he glared at his boyfriend. "Don't."

Jake decided to go for more humor. "When a man and a man love each other very much, there comes a time when they want to give in to their urges."

"Oh my God, Uncle Jakey, you're making it worse." Jericho's glare turned in his direction. "That's not it."

"It is kinda it, boo." Jordan looked down at Jericho, a dopey expression on his face that Jake had seen hundreds of times in his own mirror. "You wanted to make sure your uncle daddies weren't going to be upset if I take you to the hotel suite I reserved."

"They're not my uncle daddies." Jericho's face was crimson, color spreading in bright splotches up his neck and into his cheeks. "Don't do that."

"Are you going to be safe and responsible?" Jake fought his smile when Jericho jerked around to stare at him. "I can get you some of Uncle Trent's condoms if you need me to. If you're going to be safe and responsible, then there's no one I'd rather see you with than Jordie." He leaned forwards, elbows to his knees. Ignoring Jordan's stunned expression, Jake focused on Jericho. "I've loved you since I met you, son. Since before, actually. Just hearing your name on a phone call from Knoxville that turned our lives upside down, I've loved you. Do you really think I'd support you being with a man without him being worth all that's you? Jordan's the real deal, and I called it years ago when I told you he was one of the good ones. Now." He leaned back, fingers laced across his stomach, legs stretched out to prop his feet on the coffee table. "Was there anything specific you wanted to know? I can show you some videos—"

"Nooooo." Jericho's screech cut him off and made him laugh.

"You wake up the twins, and you won't be going anywhere." Jake dropped his chin and stared meaningfully under his brows at Jericho. "And if Trent heard that, you better be prepared for a longer lecture than I've provided." Jericho shifted and looked up at Jordan, who hadn't taken his gaze off Jericho's face. "Go. Go on. Be safe, and be kind to each other. That's all anyone can ever ask for."

A moment later, Jericho was standing in front of him, and Jake pushed to his feet, arms around this boy who had taught him how to be the best father he could hope to be, holding him tight. Fighting tears, he took in several careful breaths until he felt strong enough to whisper, "Love you, son."

"Love you too, Uncle Jakey." Jericho's voice didn't sound any steadier than his, and Jake fought tears again. One of Jericho's hands dropped away, and Jake knew when he looked, he'd find the boys' fingers linked, a clasp so intrinsic to their relationship he wondered sometimes if they even knew they did it.

"Go on." He stepped back but didn't turn away, not afraid to let Jericho see how moved he was. "I'll see you tomorrow?" Jordan nodded at him over Jericho's shoulder.

Watching them walk through the house and into the garage, he stared at the closed door for a long time. Long enough that Trent descending the stairs was a surprise, jolting him back into movement.

"Jakey, is everything okay?" Bundled into a robe Jericho had gotten him last Christmas, Trent tugged on the ends of the tie holding it closed. "Are you crying?" Hustling to stand in front of him, Trent loomed over Jake, both hands lifted and cradling his jaw. "Honeybuns?"

"Good tears, promise." He reached up and gripped one of Trent's wrists, slipping his hand into place against his husband's palm, feeling their fingers fall through, interweaving and holding on. He led the way to the couch, arranging himself so Trent could curl on his side, head in Jake's lap. Clasped hands pressed over Trent's heart, tight enough Jake could feel the steady thump under the skin and bone, he relaxed back and sighed.

"Jordan took Jericho to a hotel for the night."

"Jordie did what?" Trent's cry echoed through the room, interrupted a moment later by a warbling wail Jacob identified as Lottie. That was quickly joined by Jack's stronger cries.

"And just like that, you've proved that a response of 'babe' is sometimes the best way to go."

"How can you be so calm? Jericho's our baby boy." Trent struggled up onto one elbow, gaze fixed to Jacob's face. Jake recognized the feigned annoyance in Trent's expression and grinned.

"Babe."

THANK YOU SO MUCH FOR READING *Bet On Us!*

I truly hope you enjoyed this sweet story built around characters we first saw in the *With My Whole Heart* world. If you haven't yet read Jaime and Connor's story of coming together, be sure to check it out!

books2read.com/wholeheart

ABOUT THE AUTHOR

Raised in the south, *Wall Street Journal* & *USA TODAY* bestselling author MariaLisa learned about the magic of books at an early age. Every summer, she would spend hours in the local library, devouring books of every genre. Self-described as a book-a-holic, she says "I've always loved to read, but then I discovered writing, and found I adored that, too. For reading...if nothing else is available, I've been known to read the back of the cereal box."

Want sneak peeks into what she's working on, or to chat with other readers about her books? Join the Facebook group! **bit.ly/deMora-FB-group**

deMora's got a spam-free newsletter list she'd love to have you join, too: **bit.ly/mldemora-newsletter**

~~~~~
~~~~~

Also by MariaLisa deMora

Alace Sweets, a dark romantic suspense standalone

A dark thriller, this book is not a light read. Filled with edge-of-your-seat suspense, this intense story commands the reader's attention as it drives towards the explosive ending. Alace Sweets is a vigilante serial killer, with everything that implies and is sure to trip all your triggers. Be ready.

At seventeen, Alace Sweets turned a corner in her life, taking the wrong shortcut home from school.

Resisting the harsh knowledge her attackers will never be made to pay for their actions, Alace takes a stand. Justice must be served, and if fate's scales are out of balance, she's determined to set things right as best she can.

When the laws of men fail, the rules of Alace prevail.

5-Star Reviews for Alace Sweets

"Whatever deep dark trench [deMora] pulled a character like Alace from should be revisited again and often."
~Confessions of a Serial Reader

"deMora has a superb story-line and exceptional character development. All of her characters have such depth that will intrigue the reader..."
~Turning Another Page

"Hot, sweet, dark thriller."
~Beth D

"It will keep you on the edge of your seat and give you chills."
~Escape Reality Book Blog

"Disturbing, haunting, sickly; yet hot, sexy and heart racing!"
~Amanda L

"From the first page [deMora] pulls you into the world she has created and you do not even try to escape..."
~Little Shop of Readers Blog

"A must read for all those dark, gritty romance fans out there."
~Sweet & Spicy Reads

"You will find yourself so drawn into the story that the outside world is blocked out and your locking the doors and turning on all the lights."
~Danena F

"Don't judge me for bonding with a vigilante serial killer, she's more than what she does."
~iScream Books

"Thrilling...chilling...full of suspense, nail biting edge of your seat excitement."
~Tracey H

"Every time MariaLisa deMora picks up her pen (or opens her computer), she creates characters you want to believe in."
~Gail S

"Intriguing dark storyline, beautiful love story and nail-biting conclusion, what more could a reader ask for?"
~Manda M

"This book takes you a dark and twisted ride that is gripping..."
~Renee Entress' Blog

"This book is dark and gritty and I literally had to take a day off from reading it because it's that intense."
~My Girlfriend's Couch

"This is my favourite book so far from this author ... I recommend this book if you enjoy dark romantic thrillers."
~Cheekypee Reads and Reviews

"There's not enough stars to give this book and 5 just doesn't really do it justice!"
~DeLane C

"I couldn't put this book down from page one! Tried to stop & go to bed but couldn't sleep thinking about Alace and got up & finished the book."
~Debbie M

"MariaLisa DeMora, wordsmith that she is, made this a story of the enlightenment of a woman and finding love in a life where she has had none."
~Kat W

~~~~~
~~~~~

Hard Focus, a criminal thriller standalone

This is an intense page-turner, a gut-punch twist-filled story about a woman who has confidence in herself, believes she's a good judge of character, and has filled her life with people she can trust. She's right, but she's also very, very wrong. Readers will have a time of it trying to decide who to watch closest.

Where do you place your trust when your own instincts betray you?

Connie Rowe is a receptionist at a respected legal firm. She's a little bit sassy, a lotta bit happy, has good friends, and is adored by her neighbors.

Life is good.

She's got a boyfriend she enjoys spending time with. He can be a little intense, but he's got a lot going on in his own life, sorting out his young daughter and nightmare of an ex.

Life is grand.

"Trust your gut." That's what Connie's police officer father told her often, training his daughter to believe in herself through the years.

But ... what happens when you can't? When your intuition lies?

What happens when things come into Hard Focus?

5-Star Reviews for Hard Focus

"Hard Focus is one very well-written tale. 5 stars is not enough for me."
~Tabitha

"What a powerful story. [deMora] kept me invested from the first word to the last."
~Jesse R

"[deMora] has a certain magical touch to writing her characters, that they become either your nemesis, your best friend, or your love interest. That is certainly portrayed in this spin around. Loved it, loved it, loved it."
~Sandy K

"I strongly recommend this book for both entertainment and to broaden your knowledge of certain laws that must be revisited."
~Words Turn Me On

"A intense page turner. Once you start, you can't put the book down."
~Tracey H

"A beautifully written, powerful read that I can't rate highly enough. This story will stay with me always."
~Gayle

"This book had twists I didn't see coming. Loved it!"
~Lori R

"Wow! I am in awe of deMora's skill in crafting this story."
~Kat W

"I keep sayin that there just aren't enough stars to give to some of Marialisa deMora's books...this one is no different!"
~deLane

"Where do I start with this one...I read this in 3 1/2 hours uninterrupted, I absolutely could NOT put it down. Very deep, keeps you guessing, what's gonna happen next, kind of book. I love how strong her characters are, especially the females!"
~Wendy I

"Sometimes I feel like MariaLisa deMora is the one I should be watching out for. I started reading her books because I'm addicted to MC Romance, but then she decides to change things up and I just follow her wherever she leads me like a Pied Piper. I never know what to expect, and sometimes I'm afraid to find out, but it's always an adventure."
~Rosa for iScream Books Blog

"A plot full of twists and turns, a story that's not quite what it seems, strong characterization, jaw dropping revelations... what more do you need from a book?"
~Manda M

"This book kept me turning the pages wondering what was going to happen. I am usually pretty good at guessing twists but not with this book. She totally surprised me and brought me out of my funk. 5 stars."
~Glenna M

"What an amazing story! Filled with a smidge of suspense, a dash of action and a heap of realism of our country's laws and how their vague application to victims can adversely affect its citizens and the people in their lives."
~Naughty Mom Story Time

Neither This Nor That MC romance series

Legends are born from moments like these. Folktales spun around a single point in time so perfect, you can almost hear the click resonating through the universe as things align. Meet Twisted, Po'Boy, Retro, and Ragman, good old boys from southern states who have many things in common. First, is a bone-deep love of the biker lifestyle. Second, would be their love of the brotherhood, and knowing that you trust the man at your back. Finally, these men have the love of a good woman. None of these come without a price, and it is our pleasure to journey along with them as they discover the blessings that can be won, and lost along the way.

This is the Route of Twisted Pain
Treading the Traitor's Path: Out Bad
Shelter My Heart
Trapped by Fate on Reckless Roads
Thunderstruck

Twisted is one of the most original and interesting characters I have read in a long time. Marialisa's character building is setting a high bar for her to follow, she will hopefully continue with Po'Boy's story. The Route of Twisted Pain was pure brilliance, and I highly recommend this read.
~Penny T.

This book obsessed me!
This may be the best book I read all year.
These people...they're not characters, they're real... have stuck in my head from the day I met them.
MariaLisa deMora can throw words down that'll Twist (hehe) your insides up till you can't breathe for waiting to hear what's next!
I'm working my way through her other 'families' and yup....she really is that good.
~DeLane

Treading the Traitor's Path: Out Bad
"Treading the Traitor's Path: Out Bad is a solidly engrossing, well-written novel by a talented author. MariaLisa deMora delivers a thrilling ride filled with exciting suspense, deliciously explicit, vivid sex scenes, and gritty, fast-paced action. Her characters are smart, complex, and strong with sharp edges. The settings meticulously detailed.
Fans of Motorcycle Club romance stories will not want to miss this second installment in deMora's exciting series."
~ NY Literary Magazine

What an amazing read! DeMora does not simply wrote a book, she pulls you into a different world. When you read her work, you are very much surrounded by the characters and setting. Prepare for a book hangover because once you finish the book, you will still be stuck with Po Boy.
~KW

THIS WAS AMAZING. Highly recommend for a good story line, interesting characters. I just wish there was more more more.
~Laura

Loved This Book!
What did I just read?! Is my kindle still working? I'm pretty sure it combusted into flames while reading this story. RED HOT READ for 2017. Not what I was expecting at all! I tend to stay away from ménage a trois, because for me it's hard to say there's any kind of conflict except for jealousy, and the ending kind of leaves things unresolved and unrealistic. NOT THIS BOOK! The best one out there guaranteed.
~Linda A

...seriously this series is just WTF so freaking good. Dark, Twisted, harsh, painful and raw. Po'Boy lives for his club, his brothers and his family, there is nothing he wouldn't do for them.
~Fay

I live and breathe for books like this! Fabulously Naughty!...Wickedly Hot! This is my first book by MariaLisa deMora and it will not be my last. MariaLisa delivered a 5 STAR READ! The plot is filled with action, suspense, romance and tons of hot scenes.
~Jenny F

~~~~~

My Rebel Wayfarers MC and the Neither This Nor That MC series do cross over, along with the Occupy Yourself band books, so readers have a couple of choices. The series can be read independently beginning with RWMC, OYBS, and then NTNT without too many spoilers. There's also a crossover between my RWMC world and Lila Rose's Hawks MC world. Or they can be read intertwined—in chronological order.

Here's the recommended reading order if you want to follow according to timing:

Mica, RWMC #1

A Sweet & Merry Christmas, RWMC #1.5

Slate, RWMC #2

Bear, RWMC #3

Born Into Trouble, OYBS #1

Jase, RWMC #4

Gunny, RWMC #5

Mason, RWMC #6

Hoss, RWMC #7
~~~~~

This Is the Route of Twisted Pain, NTNT #1

Harddrive Holidays, RWMC #7.5

Duck, RWMC #8

Biker Chick Campout, RWMC #8.5

Watcher, RWMC #9

Treading the Traitor's Path: Out Bad, NTNT #2

Living Without, Lila Rose's Hawks MC: Caroline Springs #4

Shelter My Heart, NTNT #3

A Kiss to Keep You, RWMC #9.25

Gun Totin' Annie, RWMC #9.5

Secret Santa, RWMC #9.75

Trapped by Fate on Reckless Roads, NTNT #4

Bones, RWMC #10

Gunny's Pups, RWMC #10.25

Not Even A Mouse, RWMC #10.75

Road Runner's Ride, RWMC #12.5

Never Settle, RWMC #10.5

Fury, RWMC #11

Christmas Doings, RWMC #11.25

Gypsy's Lady, RWMC #11.5

Thunderstruck, NTNT #5

Going Down Easy

No Man's Land

Cassie, RWMC #12

~~~~~
~~~~~

ADDITIONAL SERIES AND BOOKS

Please note that books in a series frequently feature characters from additional books within that series. If series books are read out of order, readers will twig to spoilers for the other books, so going back to read the skipped titles won't have the same angsty reveals.

Rebel Wayfarers MC series:

Mica, #1
A Sweet & Merry Christmas, #1.5
Slate, #2
Bear, #3
Jase, #4
Gunny, #5
Mason, #6
Hoss, #7
Harddrive Holidays, #7.5
Duck, #8
Biker Chick Campout, #8.5
Watcher, #9
A Kiss to Keep You, #9.25
Gun Totin' Annie, #9.5
Secret Santa, #9.75
Bones, #10
Gunny's Pups, #10.25
Never Settle, #10.5
Not Even A Mouse, #10.75
Fury, #11
Christmas Doings, #11.25
Gypsy's Lady, #11.5
Cassie, #12
Road Runner's Ride, #12.5

Occupy Yourself band series:

Born Into Trouble, #1
Grace In Motion, #2 (TBD)
What They Say, #3 (TBD)

Neither This, Nor That MC series:

This Is the Route Of Twisted Pain, #1
Treading the Traitor's Path: Out Bad, #2
Shelter My Heart, #3
Trapped by Fate on Reckless Roads, #4
Thunderstruck, #5

Rebel Wayfarers & Incoherent MC (NTNT) crossover stories:

Going Down Easy
No Man's Land

Mayhan Bucklers MC series:

Most Rikki-Tik, #1
Mad Minute, #2
Pucker Factor, #3
Boocoo Dinky Dau, #4 (TBD)

Borderline Freaks MC series:

Service and Sacrifice, #1
More Than Enough, #2
Lack of Inbetween, #3
See You in Valhalla, #4

**If You Could Change One Thing:
Tangled Fates Stories**

There Are Limits, #1
Rules Are Rules, #2
The Gray Zone, #3

Other Books:

With My Whole Heart
Bet On Us
Alace Sweets
Hard Focus
Dirty Bitches MC: Season 3

More information available at **mldemora.com**.